Praise for—

Ben Armstrong's Strange Trip Home

David Allan Cates ignites a new vision of Cain and Abel. Invitingly mysterious and breathtakingly compelling—the story takes on the shape of a rattling tale. Although the story is dreamlike, it does not stall or coerce like a dream—it opens out to mythic possibilities, the strange truths of life. There is a deep hunger for literature that expresses desire and fear with fearlessness and David Allan Cates is on that cutting edge. Wonderful—an *Alice in Wonderland* journey for grown-ups.

—Debra Magpie Earling, *author of Perma Red*

David Allan Cates may take you places you've never been, have never imagined going—to a dead brother slowly turning into a fish on your staircase landing, say, or into the fields around your house only to find a ghost troop of Union soldiers encamped there—but his great knowledge of the deep workings of the human heart serves as an unerring guide wherever his story leads. This is a deeply moving work by an uncannily gifted writer.

—Pete Fromm, author of *Indian Creek Chronicles,* and *How all this Started*

X Out of Wonderland

At once a swipe at capitalism run amok, a brilliant narrative of one man's optimism in the face of misfortune and an example of how a writer can take on big themes without overlooking fiction's obligation to offer compelling characters.

—*Kansas City Star*

A biting satire of modern capitalism . . . Cates delivers a caustic but never cynical take on what he sees as the demoralizing fatalism implicit in today's market-mad ideology.

—*Publishers Weekly*

It takes a brave writer to tackle all of it—the complete and crushing madness of our time. It takes an extraordinarily talented writer to succeed. *X Out of Wonderland* is a smart bomb guided by laser wit.

—Richard Manning

A witty, skillful, amusing—and unrelentingly clear-eyed satire.

—*Kirkus*

Freeman Walker

A magnificently absorbing novel, one that subtly, yet definitively, resonates with the highly politicized tenor of our current times . . .
—*Missoula Independent*

Historical fiction? Bildungsroman? Picaresque? How about all three . . . and then some. It's a dandy travel book taking us through mid-19th Century America and England. It's a funny coming-of-age for a half-slave, half-freedman. It's crammed with characters from London, America, the battlefields, the graves, the old west: A father who carries the *Declaration of Independence* around in his pocket, a Jewish thief who always leaves half of the loot behind (in case his victims might need it), the Irish Colonel Cornelius O'Keefe, who led one of the many uprisings against the English.
—*The Review of Arts, Literature, Philosophy and the Humanities*

What Freeman Walker sees is the untidy, complicated soul of an America that wants to believe in its innocence despite evidence to the contrary.
—*Missoulian*

Hunger in America

This is a fine work of fiction . . . by a serious and very gifted writer.

--*New York Times*

David Cates's first novel, once read, becomes even more mysterious and haunting upon contemplation. The riddle of fate is beautifully posed.

—*Los Angeles Times*

A multilayered odyssey, it is a profound exploration of life's uncertainty and the nature of spiritual hunger . . .

—*Chicago Sun-Times*

This is big-shouldered prose. It steams and geysers. It avalanches and floats on air and water. It bites and munches and goes to suspension. It's the calling card of a new American writer.

—Robert Olmstead, author of *Coal Black Horse*

Cates's first novel is solid proof that the sparest things can also be the richest...

—*Publishers Weekly*

Ben Armstrong's
Strange Trip Home

Ben Armstrong's Strange Trip Home

A novel

David Allan Cates

Novelas Americanas

Buenos Aires   Lolo   Fairbanks   New York   Spring Green   Tegucigalpa

Ben Armstrong's Strange Trip Home is a work of fiction.

Copyright © 2012 David Allan Cates

All rights reserved. No part of this book may be reproduced without written permission from the author and *Novelas Americanas*.

http://www.davidallancates.com/

Cover Design by Abe Coley

Book layout and design by Peggy Christian

Copyediting by David Colledge

Leadership: Josh Wagner

Cataloguing-in Publication Data

Cates, David Allan.

Ben Armstrong's Strange Trip Home: a novel/David Allan Cates.

ISBN 978-1470077617

1.   Homecoming—Fiction I. Title

First Edition

For Anna Marie, Margaret, and Mary Louise—
all in, always

The past is never dead. It's not even past.

William Faulkner

Forgiving yourself is a long strange tumble
toward the center of the earth.

Ben Armstrong's mom

WHEN BEN ARMSTRONG WOKE he heard the mourning dove coo in the cedar tree outside his open window. He heard cows bawling in the pasture and smelled fresh dew, yet he felt a vague dread in the marrow of his bones. Summer again? He could have sworn just last night it was fall, or maybe even winter. He blinked and looked around the familiar room. Back on the home farm after twenty-five years away, lying in his boyhood bed—no wonder he felt strange. He listened to water running downstairs, a pan banging, and a woman singing. The sounds reassured him. He smelled sausage and coffee until his stomach began to grumble, and then in a sudden boyish burst, he got out of bed and opened the bedroom door with the intent of bounding down the stairs, ready to eat.

But in a warm patch of sunlight spread across the landing at the top of the stairs, he saw something that stopped him cold. His brother lay sprawled on his back, head hanging over the top step.

'Danny?'

Danny didn't move. His big body lay limp in a white t-shirt, baggy blue jeans, and his feet were bare. Ben knelt next to him and noticed a palm-sized patch of something shiny on the side of his brother's neck. He let his fingers graze over the spot, felt the smooth texture, the overlap of scales.

'What stinks?' It was Sara Koepke, Danny's wife. She stood at the bottom of the stairs in her thick red bathrobe, looking up, wrinkling her nose. Ben was momentarily distracted by her disapproving frown, her elastic mouth. Still he managed to lay his ear down on Danny's cold chest. He heard no heartbeat but smelled a faint fish smell. He lifted his head.

'I think he might be dead,' he said.

Sara walked up the stairs and squatted beside Ben. She touched Danny's head tenderly, ran her fingers down his neck. 'Don't worry,' she said. 'It's not as if you're the first person in the world to kill his brother.'

'What?' Ben whispered. He felt slow and dizzy. Sara took his hand and helped him stand and reluctantly step over Danny's body and begin down the stairs. In the living room she handed him a handkerchief. He sat down on the couch and blew his nose. His forehead was sweating profusely so he folded the hanky and wiped his skin dry. He remembered drinking whiskey and laughing late into the night with his brother—but was that last night or years ago?

'Not remembering is probably for the best,' she said, and again he felt her hand on his. He stood and she led him without resistance down the steps to the yard and around the house through the back gate into the pasture. She was suddenly taller, slimmer, and younger. She wore bell-bottom blue jeans and a pink blouse, and he walked slightly behind her, still in his baggy boxers. He liked the way her short brown hair lay against her collar and touched her neck.

'Where are the girls?' he asked.

'Grown,' she said. 'Jessie's on the East Coast. Ivy's on the West.'

'Where are we going?'

She relaxed her grip on his hand. 'I thought after having been gone for so long, you might like to see the place again.'

'Sure, but what about Danny?'

Sara Koepke paused to look at him, her brown eyes patient. Ben felt stupid. He noticed her lipstick, red as blood. Had she been wearing it before? A puffy white cloud hung in the blue sky behind her head.

'Aren't we lucky to have such a pretty day?' she said.

Ben followed her past the wooden corncrib and into the pasture sparkling with dew. The grass grew ankle deep and thick, and as they crossed the valley, he got suddenly very cold and noticed uncountable bones scattered about. They felt hard and uncomfortable under his bare feet. He shivered.

'I never noticed these when I was a kid,' he said.

'Sure you did,' she said.

Ben decided to walk with his eyes closed and that was better, easier. He felt warm again, and heard robins and sparrows and the occasional loopy call of a meadowlark. He was a boy again, barefoot in the summer pasture. Sara walked just ahead of him and even blind he could feel her nearness.

'Why is Danny growing scales on his neck?' Ben asked, his own voice barely recognizable to him, childlike.

'He's turning into a fish,' she said.

Ben tried to think about that but didn't know how to begin. He walked fast to keep up, and after stumbling twice he opened his eyes again. Sara's arms swung from side to side as she stepped across a little creek and began to climb a hill into the woods. Ben scrambled after her. The trail was lined on either side with birches bending toward one another, making a tunnel of white and green.

'Besides not remembering killing him,' Ben said, 'there's something else I don't understand.'

Sara stopped at the edge of the forest and turned to look at him. 'What now?'

'Why would I?'

Her red lips spread to a smile and her eyes sparkled. She leaned forward and kissed Ben lightly on the lips.

'Because you love me,' she whispered. 'You always have. Don't you remember that either?'

THIS WOULD BE THE LOGICAL place to wake up if Ben Armstrong's life were a logical life and this story a mere dream. But nobody's life is logical, and because this is a true account of a real life, no dream is a mere dream. For example, it's true Ben had gone to bed in his childhood bed and in a fever began to dream and to dream again. It's true he'd come home to the farm after twenty-five years away.

But the reason he'd come home was that just the night before, while sleeping in his comfortable bed, in his house, in our nation's capital, he'd dreamed he was back on the farm, in the barn, having a sexual encounter with Sara Koepke in the body of a coyote. Or a sexual encounter with a coyote that spoke in Sara's voice. Okay, *odd* you might say. But after twenty five years away, an unsettling *dream* is what brought Ben Armstong home?

Partly, yes. But especially as it led into something even stranger. When he woke from the coyote dream, he lay on his back for a while trying to get his bearings. He still had a distracting erection and pondered for an uncomfortable moment what to do with it. He tossed off his sheet and took a deep breath. His pillow felt just right, the mattress comfortable and reassuring. He rolled over onto his side and was about to settle back into sleep when he noticed the absolute darkness—no line of streetlight coming from the around the drapes, no night-light in the hall. He blinked and raised his head, propped himself up on his elbow, which is when he saw his mother's ghost. You'd think after a weird dream he might catch a break, but there she was, a white smudge suspended in the air at the foot of his bed. He hadn't seen his mother since the summer he was five years old and she'd drowned in the slough, in a car with his father. He struggled to cover himself with a sheet.

Don't bother, she said. *I'm dead.*

He covered himself anyway. He sat up and blinked. 'You look different,' was all he could think to say.

She laughed. *I've been dead a long time.* She carried a letter from his brother that he'd read two decades ago and thrown away in bitterness and fear. She laid it open on the desk.

Danny forgives you, she said. *Don't waste that.*

At the mention of his brother's name, Ben tried to scream but no sound came out. He tried again but the effort merely lifted him three feet off his mattress, where he levitated and shuddered. His brother might have forgiven him, but what did that matter if Ben had never forgiven himself? When he came back down onto his bed he was in a terrible sweat and his mother was gone, the house quiet. Powerless to resist, he was soon standing at his lighted desk, his hands flat on the pressed leather, reading his brother's words in blue ink scrawled on white lined paper.

Dear Ben,

It's August, the month when fairies come at night to drape the hollow in fog. It's muggy, sweat weather—everything's sticky, the table, the floor. The cattle are tucked under the oaks along the fence line of South pasture. I should be mowing thistles but the tractor's in the shop. Sara said, Write your brother . . .

Ben tried to stop reading there but was intrigued by the image of Sara's face and mouth forming those words and he was unable to pull his body away from the desk. He continued:

So here I am, doing as she wills, as always, helpless . . .

Of course, Ben thought, and a lump of panic hardened in his stomach. What had continued to make him feel guilt was not only how he'd been unable to control himself but how much he'd liked it. He'd joyfully betrayed his brother over and over again. To calm himself now, he studied Danny's handwriting, a unique combination of cursive and printed letters, but he couldn't do that for long and soon the words had pulled him back in again.

The fan in the girls' room (our old room) is blowing across the hall into my green office (Grandma and Grandpa's old room). I've got a desk and a filing cabinet and a phone up here, and I can put my feet up and look out the window and watch the sun burn the fog and make the dew on the grass sparkle like soda water. Jessie has come up the stairs, sits in her room where I can see her, removes her sundress, puts on the bottom half of her

*two-piece, asks for help with the top. I swear she changes
clothes ten times a day. She says* What is my room
doing? *And* Nobody knows what I'm wearing! *Before
she leaves to go downstairs, she shows me her new shorts
and t-shirt.* Lookit, *she says.* I haven't worn it all
summer! *She has one hand on each side of the doorway,
pushes herself back and forth, her brown hair swinging
past her face, grinning.*

Ben looked up into the darkness of his room past the yellow
desk light. He knew he'd go back to the letter because there was
more, of course, much more, and the images compelled him,
painful as they were, and either way now he knew he'd have to
endure a long, sleepless night haunted by questions. How long can
a man stay away? How long before he tries to go home again? It
had been twenty-five years. Twenty-five years. Three words, but
what did they mean? His life. His *adult* life. Twenty-five years of
adulthood and what had happened? Late nights like this, sleep
coming and going, the light on, the light off, the light on again. A
series of academic and professional achievements printed in paper
and framed on his den wall. The accumulation of a large
retirement fund and of exotic vacation footage. X-rated memories
of beautiful women he'd dated doing sexy things that never seemed
to have the effect that either he or the women had hoped.
Thousands of successful orgasms bathed in general
disappointment. So much disappointment that lately, even as he

began to make love with a woman for the first time, a creeping flat feeling threatened to ruin his pleasure unless he could by force of will alone pull up the image of Sara Koepke from his youth, lying on the river beach, the hot sun heating her skin and the nylon of her suit. He read:

> *Sara and I did it on the kitchen counter early this morning. The water for the coffee was boiling. The fruit . . .*

Bastard, Ben thought. But despite the pain—or maybe because of it—he couldn't stop reading.

> *. . . the fruit she'd been chopping lay in its juice on the cutting board. There's something melancholy in the air here, yet these are not the last days of Pompeii. These are the precious days of August, the nights like cool water, the days slow and burning. The word Love seems small to me. Maybe because it's the anniversary of Grandma's funeral, but every time I see something like the hawk on the fencepost on the way down the driveway in the morning, or the shapes of the green hills folding into one another, round and soft this time of year against the pale sky—every time I see something like that it practically makes me bawl. Then the next moment I want to shout for joy.*

Jessie and Ivy are on the floor playing, Jessie in a pink sundress now, wearing new pink fingernail polish, and Ivy in a diaper and t-shirt. She started to walk this week. About ten minutes ago I caught her trying to plug in the fan. Millimeters from death, she was, her little fingers holding the copper prongs and trying to poke them into the wall socket.

Yesterday morning I walked down the pasture with Mimi the dog to separate the bull from the herd. I had a weed scythe in my hand to decapitate any stray thistles, but also to protect myself from the bull. He likes to face off with intruders. Mimi herded most of the cows back up the hollow, but I got a couple of cows to step over the fence, followed by the bull—he wasn't coming by himself, that's for sure. He's a big guy, cream-colored, and grouchy in his old age. I put him in the barn to wait for the Bull Man to come and haul him off. In the meantime, I cut some green grass and threw it down the manger, along with a coffee can of ground corn. I was feeling generous, I suppose. Later, at the river, Jessie and I walked upstream along the sandbar. Sara and Ivy stayed back. We walked quietly. A couple of times I tried to engage her by saying, Isn't this beautiful? *It's something I remember Mom and Dad saying to us about a hill, a view, the light in the sky—and something I remember not understanding. Jessie held my hand and didn't understand either. She shivered because she'd already gone swimming. The river was silver and green, a reflection of the hills and bluffs and also some algae. We got to where the river bends north, and she lay in the warm dry sand, made shapes with her arms and feet and hands. I lay about fifty feet away. Three or four hundred yards downstream toward the bridge, I could see Sara reading and Ivy's little head bobbing around her feet on the sand.*

We walked back there, and Jessie squatted with her sister and sorted through the sand and I knelt in front of Sara and kissed her. I know she's not happy, and perhaps never has been happy, and maybe if she left me she wouldn't be happy, either. This has all just begun to occur to me, that it is possible I can never make her happy, ever, and yet rather than depress me, I've lately felt an almost unbounded freedom.

When I kissed her, she made a slightly bothered face, an ingenious creation of hers whereby she shows her irritation yet also her monumental effort at controlling it. I sat up, then back, then lay all the way out in the sand. I called for my little girls to come bury their old man in sand, which they happily did.

And more, too, Ben reread through the night for the tenth, fifteenth, twentieth time, feeling the letter take him over, pull him, convince him. And on the jet plane the next morning, sipping a gin and tonic, mountains of cloud outside the window, the blue heavens above:

Remember the nights when we were kids, summertime, and the flies crawling on the screens, and the fan on, and the radio maybe? Remember when it stormed and we thought the heavens had sucked us into the violence? Over the hill, so close before we'd see it, the clouds appeared suddenly and heavy and tumultuous, as though you could reach your hand straight up and touch the anger? As if you could run up the hill and get pegged squarely between the eyes? And remember on calm, green, whippoorwill evenings, how the dense hillsides absorbed sound, the fireflies spreading across the valley like a continuation of the stars so you wouldn't know where the sky started and the ground ended? I remember a feeling of choking, of breath so heavy and sweet with grass and manure and corn, and then the cooking smells from the kitchen, hamburger, grease, cheese, tuna, propane. I remember the white table top under the bright light, my whole adolescent body in electric anticipation of sex. Once we skinny-dipped in the river and met two pretty tourist girls. I'm sure you remember their naked bodies running like ghosts in the dark. You paired up with the Asian one, and I was with the blonde, but I couldn't even try to touch her. I don't know why. I remember walking with her down the beach to get wood for the fire, and we were naked and it was dark, but she wasn't real yet, or I wasn't, it was all imaginary, and I didn't know how to make it real. We built the fire, still naked, and I don't think I'd ever seen a real naked girl before, and here I am with one, a beauty, too, making a campfire! We went swimming, of course, splashing in the water, white-assed in the black river, chasing each other but with no possible way to actually touch. I still feel that way with Sara. I don't fight it anymore.

The house hums with fans as the day's heat settles into the hollow. The quiet beyond the window is almost eternal. This morning in the kitchen with Sara was the first time in a long time; it was sweaty and fast and she came before I did and was crying when I finished. Which made me mad so we argued very intensely for about fifteen seconds, then apologized and kissed some more. I don't understand any of it, and am at my best when I realize I don't have to. The mystery is so deep and the cover so thin that it all spills anyway, threatening to drown both of us, which is okay, I keep telling myself, okay, okay.

Brother, I know you loved Sara—maybe still do— and I know this is why you've stayed away so long—five years?—shame or fear, even missing Grandma's funeral last year. I know this and have suffered for it, of course, but I'm writing you now for the first time in how long to tell you that I miss you and would like to see you, and that as far as I'm concerned you're welcome here, come what may. Our lives have rolled along in exile for too long. We are in the middle, in the dark, and although I may have to lose everything eventually, I don't want to lose anything until I have to.

—Danny

Ben landed in the late afternoon and rented a car at the airport. *I'm on a journey toward self-forgiveness*, he almost told the woman who handed him the keys. He felt a self-congratulatory buzz as he drove west around the big city. He listened to old jazz and found the drive comforting despite the heavy traffic. Wasn't he brave to be finally coming home again? Later, he would remember how everything seemed normal until the car left the main road for the narrow blacktop, winding into the hills where the continental glacier hadn't quite reached, where hundred-thousand-year-old gullies had become deep hollows between steep wooded ridges. The hollows turned and forked, turned and forked again, and the sky itself narrowed, and he lost track of direction. He drove through barely familiar lowlands riddled with springs and spongy with marsh, past abandoned farms, crumbled cabins, towns with a tavern, a gas station and a church, past rocky ridges casting shadows different from any he'd ever seen before.

Then the bluebird sky darkened, and the bright flat picture of home—the white farmhouse and red barn—that he carried in his head was suddenly confounded under a gray sky. He checked his chest pocket for the folded letter but it was gone—had he left it on the plane? He felt feverish and shivered, and by the time he turned down the long gravel driveway into the narrow between two round hills, crossed the creek and passed the barn to park in front of the house, the leaves had colored brilliant reds and yellows and oranges, then browned and fallen, and the black trunks of oak and hickory stood on the hillsides naked as skeletons.

Sara Koepke met him at the front door, her face pale as though she were seeing a ghost. 'You?'

He felt a lump of unexpected shame and tried to swallow. 'I should have called.'

'No,' she said, and tucked a wisp of gray hair off her forehead and behind her ear. 'I'm sorry. You surprised me, Ben. Come in.'

He stepped past her and into the house for the first time in twenty-five years. It smelled of ashes and something else. The maple floor was the same. A new square woodstove replaced his grandma's old pot-belly.

'Where's Danny?'

'Fishing,' she said. 'He'll be home tomorrow.' Her voice trailed off.

Ben stared at her face, still elastic but her skin paler, lined, and with a fuzz of colorless hair on her cheeks and above her top lip. Also her unusually timid eyes. She looked weakened by life, turned somehow fragile. He had a feeling his gaze was hurting her. He shivered and looked away.

'Do you mind if I nap?' he asked.

'No. Please.' She seemed relieved. She led him across the living room toward the stairs so he could put his bag in his room. He shivered again and wondered if he'd packed enough clothes. The orange carpeted stairs creaked as they always had under his weight and without thinking he stepped slightly higher on the uneven third step to keep from tripping. The white walls in the stairwell were lined with photos of the girls growing up—but the air smelled like something had died.

'Sorry about the stink,' she said. 'There's a dead rat behind the plaster wall. We're not quite sure what to do about it.'

'It's not so bad.'

She laughed. 'Yeah, right.'

He put his bags in what was once Danny and his boyhood bedroom, Jessie and Ivy's room since then. Quickly, Sara made up one of the twin beds, folding under the mattress the fresh sheets and blankets.

'Where are the girls?'

Sara paused and looked at him, uncomprehending for a moment. 'They've grown up.'

'Oh,' Ben said, 'Of course. I just thought—' He sat on the bed and squeezed his temples with his palms. 'Forgive me,' he said. 'I guess I'm not as brave as I thought I was. Maybe I should leave this afternoon.'

'Please,' she said, reaching out as though to stop him, though he hadn't moved. He stayed seated, hands on the side of his face.

'Is everything okay?' Such concern in her voice, as though she thought he might be sick, might be coming home to die.

'No,' he said. 'I mean yes, I'm fine.' His pulse pounded in his forehead. He wished he still had Danny's letter. He wondered if he'd dreamed it all. He looked up and tried to smile.

'I'm just suddenly very tired,' he said.

She touched his shoulder and it seemed all the blood in his body raced to where her fingers lingered.

'You feel hot,' she said, 'Lie down. Sleep. Rest. Danny will be overjoyed to see you. He loved you—*loves* you. He'll be back tomorrow.'

And then, like that, her fingers withdrew. Ben's body felt limp and senseless. He waited until she left the room to lie down and crawl under the covers. He rolled on his side and shivered with a feverish chill. The pillow was thicker than his old pillow and propped his head up too high. His grandmother's old wallpaper was gone and the walls were a clean white and the woodwork and windows new. He recognized the smell of the room, though, the feel of the old mattress, and he recognized the texture of the white ceiling, even the little webs spun daily in the corners by tiny brown spiders. Familiar light streamed through the window. He and Danny had spent much of the first winter in this room killing cluster flies. Every day a hundred more were born and clustered on the window glass. And every day they killed them all, even kept a body count. Ben had had a cast on his leg and he hopped from the window to his bed and back again in the cold, double-checking Danny's count. It was the winter after the summer their parents died. The next winter there were fewer flies. And the next, none at all.

Ben pulled the blankets up to his chin and curled into a ball to stay warm.

'When you wake, I'll have dinner,' Sara called from the bottom of the stairs.

BUT WHEN BEN OPENED HIS EYES again it was morning in the farmhouse. He felt slightly hungover, his tongue swollen. His nap after his arrival yesterday afternoon had apparently stretched into a long night's sleep. He must have needed it. He thought of calling a friend back in the city just to touch base but decided he'd wait until he had something to say beside that he'd had some weird dreams. The ghost of his mother, his dead brother turning into a fish, and a pretty young version of his brother's wife giving him a kiss on the lips.

He sat up. The room looked different than it did yesterday afternoon—had the clean white walls and new windows been just another dream? The feel of Sara's fingers on his shoulder? His shivers? He took a deep breath and studied the familiar old wallpaper, the college pennants on the wall, and the poster of Henry Aaron. A thin yellow line of light came in through the door and sliced the room in two, his side and Danny's side. Danny's bed had been slept in, the covers thrown back, the pillow scrunched back against the wall, and a little pile of airplane pajamas lay on the floor. Birdsong filtered through the open window.

Ben stood up and parted the drapes to see the gable of the barn roof over the top of the garage. A red Radio Flier wagon lay tipped over in the yard and yellow daffodils bloomed along the front walk. Spring? He smelled wet soil and new grass, and he went to the bedroom door to peek cautiously out into the hallway. No dead rodent smell. No dead Danny—but across the top of the stairs lay his old black cat in a patch of sunlight. She licked her paw and used it to wipe her cheeks. He knelt down and lifted her to his face. She smelled like fish. 'Shouldn't you be dead by now?' he said, dropping her. She ran down the stairs and disappeared around the corner landing.

The stairwell was lined with framed photographs of Jessie and Ivy growing up, as it had been the afternoon before. Ben paused on his way down and studied the face of the oldest, Jessie, and he wondered . . . but couldn't tell from the pictures. Suddenly he felt dread, not only at the weirdness of seeing that old cat, but at the prospect of having to spend the morning hours in the house alone with Sara Koepke. Would he and Sara be able to talk without *that question* coming up? His heart was beating fast when he reached the bottom of the stairs. The new square woodstove was gone and his grandma's old pot-belly was back. What was going on? He crossed the living room and entered the kitchen. It was a huge relief to see Sara's note on the kitchen table. She'd let him sleep the afternoon before, she said, and this morning as well, and she hoped that after such a long rest he'd feel better. She had to run an errand, but would be back later to cook dinner. Danny was expected home by the middle of the afternoon. Ben should feel free to eat whatever he could find, sleep some more if he needed. If he felt up for it, she said, he should take a walk and swim in the big pond, as they'd made a beach on one end and anchored a little float.

Ben went to the sink, drank a big glass of water and looked through the window at the fully-leafed elm and maple in the yard. He stepped out the back door and opened the gate and walked between wood piles and past the old corncrib. The air felt hot, heavy, and still. It was full summer now and the forest on the hills looked solid and impenetrable, the valley grass grazed down from wild spring. The ponds lay almost a half mile back, just over a rise, so he took his shirt off and felt the sun on his skin and he was wet with perspiration by the time he arrived.

The first pond was the smallest, maybe a quarter acre, and in the few areas not choked with weeds, largemouth bass swam lazily in the clear water. Ben crossed the berm to the slightly bigger pond, the surface reflecting the round hills and a single puff of cloud. He took a quick swim out to the wooden float, felt the spring water bring his body to life, quicken his breath. He rested for a moment hanging onto the edge of the float. He let his head hang back and he looked at the blue sky. The physical exertion gave him a sense of innocence and well-being, and he felt glad for having left this place, for having had the courage to leave this place when he did. He felt pleased for having made something of his life, and proud for finally having the courage to come home again. He had four weeks of vacation and had spent two of them in Costa Rica and now he'd spend two here. Why not? Wasn't that what people did, came home to visit? The past was the past. The present was beautiful. He blinked into the glare of the sun off the water; he pushed the float away and began swimming on his back to the far shore. Heaven. What a fine hot day. What a glorious thing to be alive on earth, swimming in cool water.

He walked up the bank on the far end of the pond where a thin layer of yellow sand had been spread over the black muck. His feet pushed through in places, and in his irritation a thought emerged concerning his brother being too cheap to get enough sand, but he quickly resisted the thought—and just as quickly congratulated himself on his self-discipline and non-judgmental virtue.

He sat down and warmed himself on the sand. A red-tailed hawk screeched and flew circles in the small sky of the hollow.

What a strange trip home. The drive from the airport yesterday with its unsettling season changes, followed by the awkward greeting with Sara Koepke, which he'd expected, except for the sudden lethargy and heaviness that had infused his limbs. Just looking at her made him feel passive and tired. Then feverish and weak. He'd napped through the afternoon and all night long, apparently—when was the last time he'd slept so long?—before waking to see what must be the world's oldest cat asleep on the upstairs landing.

He lay back and closed his eyes and tried not to think anymore, especially about his bizarre dreams—his brother's scales, his mother the white smudge. He let his mind go and felt the sun hot on his wet skin. He'd always loved this place, this bend in the hollow, this little sky surrounded by round hills thick with forest. He loved the smell of these ponds, of the watercress, the sound of frogs, and the crazy call of the meadowlark. In his own personal creation myth, the gods created this place first. He couldn't believe it had taken him so long to come back. He'd done wrong, sure, but he'd practically been a child, and now here he was, a good and successful man, home again to visit family, a brother who loved him. Why not? What could go wrong? He breathed in, breathed out. Breathed in again and felt the sand under his body, breathed out and felt a slight breeze touch his skin.

Suddenly he heard voices, children's voices, and he opened his eyes and lifted his head to see two boys on the far side of the pond, skinny limbs shiny in sunlight. Naked, they ran among the thistles on the banks, dipped down into the shallow water and began covering themselves with mud, their faces and arms and legs. They took turns mudding up each other's backs and then began chasing each other. They shrieked and threw sticks like spears and ran around to the side of the pond where Ben lay. When they got close enough, Ben could see that one of the boys was Danny and one was him.

He started to curl up but there was nowhere to hide on the sand so he lay still. The boys hooted and ran to within a few feet of him but didn't seem to notice. Young Danny walked out into the pond and used a stick to drive a snapping turtle into the shallows by the bank, where young Ben poked it with his spear until it bit and held tight, and he lifted the spear with the ten-pound snapper hanging on the end, clamped on by its jaws, lifted it up over the bank, which is when the spear broke and the turtle fell into the ankle-deep pasture grass. *We got it, baby!* Danny yelled and the boys squealed and ran circles around the turtle. Then Danny lifted a rock as big as his head and brought it down with all of his force on the shell of the turtle. The sound echoed off the hills, a great loud POCK! Young Ben said *Again!* and Danny lifted the rock and brought it down again, POCK! and Ben squealed *It's cracked, it's dead!* Danny picked the big turtle up by the tail with two hands and started spinning circles like somebody doing the hammer throw, around and around he spun until he let it go with a shout. The turtle did an arc against the sky, turning a slow flip with a twist before ker-plunking down in the middle of the pond.

Young Ben complained, his voice thin as a reed. *I wanted turtle soup!*

Swim for it!

Danny!

The pond is *turtle soup!*

Then the boys were gone and only the sun glared off the water where the turtle had splashed. Ben waited and squinted, then lay back again and closed his eyes. The back of his eyelids turned blood red in the sunshine. He breathed slowly and deliberately. He listened to the wind in the trees on the ridges until he heard voices again and looked up. There on the far bank was Sara Koepke, no older than fifteen, standing thigh deep in the water wearing a blue two-piece, her arms sticking straight out from her dough-colored body, her puffy adolescent body, hair pale brown like dry grass. She slowly tiptoed out, deeper, deeper . . . Suddenly, from behind her, from the tall grass on the bank behind her, streaked a boy's nut-brown body, naked, his pubic hair and head hair the color of straw. Danny. He hit the edge of the bank at full speed and Sara Koepke squealed as he lanced himself out over the water in a lovely arc that mimicked the arc of the turtle just a moment before. He hit the water in the same place, sending up a plume of spray.

Danny! she yelled.

But he'd disappeared and the pond sealed over again with smooth water. She stood submerged to her chest now, her head and hair still dry, arms too, lifted parallel to the surface.

Danny? she said, her voice cautious.

Then the real scream, as he grabbed her legs underwater and pulled, because her head went down, and her arms, and when she came up again, they were embracing, their heads close, her white arms around his brown shoulders.

Danny! she said, giggling wildly. *Would you stop!* But Danny pulled her under again, both of their heads gone in a splash and under for some time. How long? Ben scanned the pond from the cattails on one bank to the willows on the other, and then back again to the cattails, where two smooth wet heads had reemerged and now seemed to float quietly on the smooth surface of the pond, mouths attached in a kiss.

Ben closed his eyes again and lay back on the sand and saw the colors behind his eyelids spill into one another. He tried to recapture the feeling of well-being he'd had when he first climbed out of the pond, but that seemed to have been replaced by an almost sour dread. He'd come home because the pull of love was too strong to resist any longer. His brother's love as expressed in the letter. Yet he hadn't even seen his grown brother again except in a dream as a dead man growing scales on his neck. And the love he was feeling since being home felt more and more like the frightening passion he'd felt for Sara. He had an urge to turn over and put his head into the sand but managed to convince himself that this must be a dream, too, of course. For on the bank not far from where he imagined his own feet to be, he heard his own young man's voice.

Never! he was saying. *Never!*

Then her voice, a murmur, followed by *Just . . . shut . . . up.*

Never! he said. *I could never do it!*

Don't talk, she said.

Never! he said.

Hush.

Never ever never ever!

Please, she said, her voice tender and seductive. Then silence, finally. Only the trickle of the spring into the pond. The screech of a hawk. Then the sound of scuffling, and Ben knew—remembered?—that she was pulling her clothes off and his too in joyful frenzy, and he felt ashamed to look but unable to resist. He opened one eye slightly and saw a very blue sky and then, lower, a very bare Sara (except for a baby blue camisole pulled up to her chin) lying on her back. He closed his eyes but heard the sounds of lovemaking begin and he squinted one eye open. He saw his own face—much younger, thinner—and seeing it startled him, so he closed his eye again and swallowed. The sounds continued and he dared to open his eyes again. He saw himself kneeling, holding Sara Koepke's hips up and delivering himself with a slow urgency until a sudden joy lit up the flesh of his neck and face like a flame. Carried away, his young self burst into laughter and fell back onto the grass.

Help us! he shouted at the sky. *We're in love!*

Ben closed his eyes again to silence. Only the trickle of water and a gust of wind in the box elder along the creek. He tried to catch his breath but felt as if he himself had been making love and collapsed in joyful exhaustion, his face flushed, every bare inch of his skin tingling madly. He rested, unreasonably happy, breathing deeply through his nose. He thought he felt the warmth of another close to his cheeks. He thought he smelled the skin of a woman. He watched the colors behind his eyelids change and darken. He felt breath tickle his ear, then a voice, her voice:

'Come,' she said. 'I want to show you something.'

He opened his eyes and young Sara was dressed and bending over him. 'What?' But she didn't speak again, only took his hand and pulled until he sat up. He looked around and his young self was gone.

'This way,' she said, her lipstick blood red again. He stood and followed her. They walked across the pasture and up into the woods. It was evening but still light and she was wearing blue jeans and a pink blouse, and he walked slightly behind her still in his baggy boxers. He liked the way her short brown hair lay against her collar and touched her neck. They walked for a long time, and although it grew too dark to see her he could feel her near. His blood moved to the side of him that she was on. She was the moon and his blood was the sea. Perhaps he did love her?

'Told you so,' she said.

She'd read his mind. Why not? 'I'm dreaming,' he said.

'No,' she said. 'I am.'

That figured, he thought, for he'd never dreamed a dream so full of nuance, nor one that seemed to last so long, nor one in which his legs got so tired. He wanted to sit down and rest.

'Is Danny really dead?'

'What do you think?' She turned and looked back over her shoulder but all he saw was the outline of her shape in the dark, which thrilled him.

'Impossible,' he said. How could a brother-killer feel such joy? 'I could never do it.'

She looked at him sadly. 'I've heard that before.'

They emerged from the forest path into a clearing and stood side-by-side gazing at a hillside meadow blinking with yellow lights. He paused to catch his breath. Twinkling hillsides, twinkling heavens, everything beautiful, yet his brother . . . *dead*? How could it all fit? Ben felt vertigo. As though she knew it, Sara took his hand and led him through the pasture around a grassy knoll to a dark barn. They entered a sliding door and smelled the dry manure and the old oak beams. He'd played here as a boy. He'd slept here the night his parents died. Sara spread out a blanket on the hay and lay down with her back to him. He knelt next to her and looked carefully at her face. He felt frightened and off balance and, as if to steady himself, he leaned down to kiss her. But before he could, she rolled away and tucked tighter into a ball.

'I'm tired,' she said. 'And didn't you tell me you were tired, too?'

He had, and he was, so he slept. And miraculously when he opened his eyes again he was in the very same place, looking at the graceful curve of Sara's shoulder and back, at the valley of her waist, then past her sleeping body to a pigeon feather drifting down from a beam above, passing through shafts of yellow sunlight slanting between the vertical plank walls of the barn. He knew it was true that he loved her. He couldn't recall having met her, nor when this feeling started, but he knew it was deep and old, and although his mind might have forgotten, the cells of his body had not.

Then he remembered his brother Danny, and Sara's claim that he'd killed him. He didn't believe her, couldn't—because he was a good person, and if he'd done something bad, well, wouldn't he feel bad? *You can't imagine how he's grieved.* Wouldn't Ben grieve, too? Of course he would. He was an innocent man and he'd prove it. True, he had a vague feeling of guilt for the way he loved Sara Koepke, a memory of having taken some oath to stay away from her—*never ever never ever!*—and yet here he was, lying next to her in the barn where he'd played as a boy. Climbed on those beams, swung from that rope. Lay right here on this prickly hay and looked up at that old hanging hayfork, gilded with cobwebs, under the cupola . . .

He moved over to smell, just to smell, Sara's skin. His breath woke her. She turned over and he could see her face was old again—his age, even older—but still he tried to kiss her as he'd tried last night, and again she slipped away like air.

'No no no,' she said, teasingly. 'Your brother isn't even buried yet! And besides, if you've forgotten how much you love me, you'll just have to remember again.'

'What?'

'Let's go! This way!' She was suddenly standing at the big hanging door, her face turned to that of a coyote—yellow dancing eyes, white canines, pink tongue. She smiled and beckoned him. Behind her the dark green leaves of the ash tree made a pool of shade in the long grass. She disappeared. He got up to chase her, stepped through the barn door, ran around the corner past the milk house and bumped squarely into an old woman with thinning gray hair and eyes black as night. He was afraid he'd knock her down but instead he was the one who fell. She was giant! She reached down with brown hands to pull him easily to his feet.

'Stand up, boy,' she said, bending to kiss his cheek. She smelled familiar, but he pulled back, startled.

IF BEN ARMSTRONG WERE NOT so fully aroused and chasing a changed Sara Koepke out of the barn, this might be a place where he'd like to stop this nonsense and go back to the regular world. For wasn't Sara a woman, and not a coyote? And wasn't she his brother's wife? And wasn't this old woman bending to kiss his cheek his *grandmother*?

But the decision to go back to the regular world assumes the existence of such a place, assumes that it waited solidly on the other side of a line that he could step neatly over. It's true Ben had come home again to the farm where he'd grown up, to the place he'd fled twenty-five years before in guilt and disgrace. That much anybody could agree on. It's true he greeted a woman he'd once loved clear to madness, and that he waited anxiously to see the forgiving brother he'd betrayed. None of that was complicated or confusing. He'd felt feverish; he'd gone to bed. The bed was real. The pillow. The light from the window. The foul smell of the air. Who could deny these things?

Yet the fallacy of a world divided by clean lines is as simple as this: much of what Ben knew, he'd done. And much of what he'd done, he remembered. And much of what he remembered, he'd dreamed or been told. And much of what he dreamed or been told, he knew and did and remembered and dreamed again. So the lines between what he *remembered* and *dreamed* and *been told* and *done* and *knew* turned out to be no lines at all. And the boundaries between *where-he-lives-now* and *where-he-used-to-live*, between *who-he'd-become* and *who-he'd-once-been*, between *who-he-once-loved* and *who-he-still-loves* turned out to be no boundaries at all.

This was a trip home, after all, and where has it ever been written that such trips are easy?

So just imagine how confused Ben must have felt running into his grandmother, dead for more than twenty years. How curious it must have been to feel his body suddenly small again, a child, as he bounced off of his grandmother and looked up at her. She looked sternly down at him as he fumbled with his erection through his shorts.

'Don't play with yourself,' she said. 'You'll grow scales on your hands.'

'Where did Sara go?' His voice was a little boy's voice.

Grandma wore denim overalls and a gray t-shirt. She'd been taking laundry off the clothesline and folding it into a basket. The wind tossed a line of lovely white diapers. Little socks. White sheets. 'Who?'

'Sara Koepke.'

'Playing with your brother, I suppose,' she said.

'Danny?'

'Who else?'

'But he's dead!'

His grandmother's black eyes opened wide and her mouth pursed closed. 'Well, that explains it,' she said.

'Explains what?'

'Why he sounded so distant on the phone.' She laughed and picked up the laundry basket and went into the house. Ben followed her through the kitchen and into the first floor bedroom. Pretty light filtered through the drapes. The clean sheets were folded neatly in squares. Dust danced in the shafts of light from the window. She handed Ben a sheet that smelled of sunshine.

'Take hold there,' she said.

He did, and they unfolded the sheet and spread it across the mattress. They tucked it in and lay another sheet across the bed, and then a blanket and a bedspread. Grandma picked up the basket and left the bedroom and crossed the living room and started up the stairs. Ben followed, but she stopped so suddenly he collided face-first against her denim rear end.

'Oh marvelous,' she said. 'Would you look at that.'

'What?' Ben was afraid to look.

'That!'

He bravely peeked around her bottom into the hallway, past the railing at the top of the stairs, to the far window and the sunshine spilling in and making a yellow square of light that illuminated clearly a fish's head. Ben tucked his head back into her loose overalls, then peeked out again. A half dozen large-mouth bass hung on a stringer from the railing. His grandmother gave a squeal of joy and clapped her hands.

'Your grandpa must have left them here.' She lifted the stringer into the full sunlight pouring through the hallway window. The cluster of hanging fish turned this way and that. 'Pretty, aren't they?'

'They are,' Ben said, and just a short time later he sat at the kitchen table still in his shorts, his bare feet not touching the polished maple floor while his grandmother cooked the fish.

'Where's Danny?'

'Quit nagging about Danny, will you? He's a big boy. He's out playing pirate. He's conquering distant lands.'

'I'm not hungry.'

'Suit yourself,' she said. 'Sit there and be a pill if you want. I'm going to eat this fish and I'm going to tell you a long story.'

'About what?'

'About how you got here.'

'Oh.'

The kitchen was hot and smelled of the fish sizzling in the fry pan.

'It smells.'

Grandma laughed. 'You think so?'

'I won't eat it. I think the fish is Danny.'

'Okay, don't eat if you don't want to. But don't open your mouth and let out everything that's inside your head. Nobody will know what you're talking about.'

Ben sat still, forcibly keeping his mouth closed. His eyes, too, wishing he could close his nose. If Danny came back then Ben could eat. But only then. Only if he saw Danny in the flesh.

Grandma's bottom swayed back and forth as she scraped the fry pan with the spatula. The back of her neck gleamed with perspiration. When she finished cooking, she sat down with a plate, and a fried fish on the plate, and the fish still had its head, and Ben watched her fork off a piece of white fish flesh, white as cream, flaky as pastry, and he watched her put it into her red slippery mouth and begin to chew.

'Don't look at me while I eat,' she said. 'Go to the window and try to imagine the world past your nose.'

Ben slid off his chair and walked over to the window. He had to stand on his tiptoes but he pressed his face to the screen and looked from the swing set and the wooden corncrib to the hillside covered with oak and hickory in the first green blush of spring. He had a vague memory that just this morning it had been summer. No matter. Behind him he could hear his grandma ask if he was ready, and he said yes. He searched the cool blue sky, and smelled earthworms and new grass, and the pasture across the creek looked smooth and clean in this month before the thistle and the chicory begin to grow.

'Many years ago,' his grandmother began, and the big woodsy ridge suddenly bloomed orange and yellow with autumn. The sky turned gray and a wind whipped clusters of red sumac along the fence line. Ben felt a vague panic in the blood that comes with the first scent of winter, the promise of winter in the light, the smell of squash and potatoes, of dying grass . . . He turned around. His grandmother was still behind him but no longer eating fish. She was eating French toast. She ate each bread slice with three easy moves. One to cut the slice into two pieces, two to fold and fork, and three to lift the folded piece into her mouth. She used the last slice to clean her plate of all remaining syrup. She lifted the soggy piece, plopped it across her tongue and miraculously closed her mouth around it.

'*Many years ago* what?' Ben asked.

'Many years ago,' she began again, gesturing for him to turn around and look out the window, 'many years ago your grandpa saw some terrible things. His father—your great-grandfather Clarence—was an uncommonly cruel man. Massacred my own mother's family and for many years slept happily under a blanket lined with scalps. Big hero. He made your grandpa sleep under the same blanket even though it horrified him.'

Ben stood with his chin on the windowsill again. He couldn't figure out why the window was so high, so big, why he had to stretch to see out.

'Thank goodness for death,' said Grandma, 'because old man Clarence finally died and your grandpa burned the blanket out behind the house—I swear the grass still doesn't grow in that patch beyond the old cistern under the ash trees. Have you noticed?'

'No, Grandma.'

'Here, stand on this box. Step up and press your little nose to the screen and close your eyes.'

Ben closed his eyes and thought he heard something in the wind.

'What's that screaming?'

Grandma let her fork clank onto her plate. 'Could be anything,' she said. 'Could be Indians dying in the bone cave. Could be the Screaming Woman. Did I ever tell you those stories?'

'No, Grandma.' Even on the little box, Ben had to stand on his tiptoes to keep his nose pressed against the screen. He smelled chamomile. He opened his eyes to see the sky darken and night pass over the eastern hills and spread across the valley like a blanket. He felt his thumb in his mouth. He pulled it out to speak.

'Grandma, are Mommy and Daddy dead?'

No answer. Only the wind through the leaves in the dark yard. When he could no longer endure his grandmother's silence, he asked, 'Is Danny?'

She laughed a high-pitched laugh, right behind him. 'No,' she said. 'Don't worry. Danny likes to fish with Grandpa. They went fishing this morning.'

The wind had stopped and fireflies flickered down the valley all the way to the sky, where their twinkling mingled with the stars. He held tightly to the windowsill to keep his balance.

'Where are we?'

'Feels like the center of the earth to me,' Grandma said. 'All the ghosts hanging around.'

He could feel her move close to him, then hear her kneel on the floor next to him. He felt her words on his neck, smelled the after-dinner cigar on her clothes. Outside it was morning suddenly but the sun still hadn't shown its face. Gray sky hung in the hollow and moved like a living thing.

Grandma took a deep breath before saying, 'Do you understand, boy?'

He didn't, of course. He didn't even know for sure what *understand* meant but nodded anyway because he did know that his parents had died in the river, their car having plunged into the slough on a late summer night, and now he lived there all the time. He closed his eyes and smelled his grandmother's sweat as she folded him to her bosom and carried him upstairs to bed.

WHEN BEN ARMSTRONG WOKE he was back in the farmhouse, back in a warm bed in his childhood bedroom. Even the million dust motes sparkling in the yellow beam of sunshine pouring through the window looked familiar. He got up slowly, tiptoed to the window and saw the gabled barn roof rising beyond the garage. He looked below at the tipped-over red Radio Flyer wagon on the green grass. No daffodils. He heard robins chirping, killdeer, and then he heard something behind him in the hallway. A muffled breathing, something moving. He crept bravely to the door and cracked it, eyed the hallway, and there at the far end stood Sara with her back turned, older, her hair gray and the skin of her shoulders freckled under a bright yellow sundress.

'What smells?' he asked.

She turned and gave him a curious look; he loved her face and its exaggerated expressions, even the way she tilted her head like a confused dog.

'You don't remember?'

'No.'

Ben walked farther out into the hallway. The smell was worse. He hoped it was a dead rat. Sara Koepke hadn't moved but then suddenly she did. 'Look,' she said, and when she stepped aside Ben could see his brother's body lying across the orange shag carpet on the landing. Danny's mouth stretched wide and gaped open, his lips had paled and hardened. His nose had flattened to two holes, eyes turned to gold and slipped to each side of his massive head. Nothing remained of Danny's clothes or straw-colored hair, and gaping vents exposed pink gills where his neck and shoulders had been. His arms had become fins, the fingers gone, and his two legs had merged into one broad fish tail that curled upward where the floor met the wall.

Sara stepped over him to raise the window sash and lovely summer air rushed into the stuffy hallway. 'Look,' she said. 'It's summer and the sky is blue and we live on God's green planet Earth. Look!'

But Ben had collapsed to his knees and his throat choked with grief. He'd been all over the world on vacations. On the walls of his house in our nation's capital, he had photos of himself standing next to Bedouins and Andean peasants, Eskimos and jungle chiefs, yet already this trip home was the strangest trip he'd ever taken.

'Don't worry,' Sara whispered in his ear, giving him shivers. 'I have a plan and nobody will ever know what you did.'

Ben felt the full shock of what he had done in his stomach and his throat. He couldn't look away from Danny, and Danny blurred behind tears.

'I just don't know,' he said.

Sara touched his hair above his ear, sending goose bumps racing across his skin. 'Don't worry,' she said. 'It's better not to remember. It's the way we can live happy. I should know! I've lived many unhappy years remembering, but now that your brother is dead I can finally forget. We'll be happy. We'll forget the unpleasant things.'

Ben was suddenly aware of wearing only boxer shorts. He kept his face in his hands to hide his sudden tears and leaned forward over his knees.

'But what will we do?' he asked

'Don't be silly!' Sara scolded, her fingers lingering in his hair. 'We'll eat! We'll swim!' She slapped him on the ass. 'Great recreational opportunities await us!'

He remained folded over, hidden. He prayed to wake up from this nightmare.

'Oh, come on,' Sara said, pulling at his elbow now, trying to make him sit up. 'It's not as if your brother and I were so terribly close. And you hadn't seen him in twenty-five years.'

'But he loved you,' Ben said. 'And I loved him.'

Sara Koepke's hands stopped pulling at his elbow. Her voice softened.

'Well, soon he'll be all fish, and we'll be able to haul him out of here and release him into the river he loved so well.'

'The river?'

'Yes,' she said. 'I've been checking the Internet, gathering information on what to do, how to dispose of a family member turning into a fish.'

'What?'

'Stand up.'

Ben looked up but the sunlight was behind her and he had to squint. She took his hand and pulled him to his feet and down the hallway and into Danny's office. She sat down in front of the computer and began typing.

'Look,' she said.

Ben knelt behind her. He could smell her hair and her skin, and then, suddenly, pancakes and sausage downstairs.

'I'll click on *Dead*, see?'

But Ben didn't know what he was looking at on the computer screen, which kept switching. The smells had made his mouth begin to water.

'Now I'll click on *Brother*, see?' She tapped the screen with her forefinger to show him.

'Yes.'

'Now on *Fish*.'

'Okay.'

'It gives you everything here.'

'For what?' Ben was still confused by her smells, by the sausage smells downstairs, and his dead brother's fish smell. How could he concentrate?

'It gives you what that culture does, or would do, in this situation. Here. See? It's got all the mores and customs of eight thousand cultures. Pick one.'

'Please,' Ben said. 'I don't know what you are talking about.'

'You get to pick the culture,' she said. 'For instance Zulu. How would they respond to a dead brother turning into a fish?

And the Stone Age Celts? It's got information about them. The Egyptians, the Mayans, the Blackfeet. You name it. You pick the culture and it gives you the sacred ritual you need to perform to put all of this behind you.'

'To put it behind me?'

'To begin the grieving process,' Sara said. 'And then to move on.'

'This is all too weird,' Ben said.

'But the big problem, of course, is that not many cultures have something on this specific situation. Brother-husband turning to fish. But I did find one that is similar. Oh, here. A tribe in New Guinea does, but apparently sometimes the dead bodies grow feathers, so what they do is take the feathered body and figure out what kind of bird it looks like. Then they find a nest of that kind of bird and leave the body there. That way the body will be born again.'

Ben had stopped listening. He was holding his forehead between his hands again. 'I can't believe it,' he said. 'I can't believe you and I are talking about this.'

'Oh, I know,' she said. 'I know, I know, I know. After all these years—' Her voice trailed off and she whispered, 'Me and you, finally . . . our turn.'

Ben looked up and she was smiling at him with unabashed joy. She looked beautiful but had wrinkles all over her face. How long had it been since they'd seen one another? A long time. A long, long time.

'But let's eat first,' she said, spinning around in her office chair. 'Your grandma's cooking breakfast, can you smell it?'

He did, of course. In fact his mouth was watering suddenly. 'But isn't Grandma dead?'

Sara looked at him as though he were an idiot. 'Of course she is. But listen, have you forgotten?'

'Forgotten what?'

'Today's the day it all began.'

'*What* all began?'

She stood up to leave the room and Ben watched as she stepped casually over his brother's fish body in the hallway and walked down the stairs to eat. It seemed wrong to leave his brother, but he was hungry and he followed. In the kitchen, Grandma stood over the stove. Grandpa sat at the table playing solitaire. The back door stood open and a spring breeze carried in a pink cloud of apple petals from the tree just off the stoop.

Grandma sighed, her dark eyes full of wonder as she watched hundreds of petals settle silently across the polished maple floor.

'I've had the door open all morning just waiting for that!' she said.

Sara walked barefoot across them as if she hadn't just stepped over her dead husband upstairs in the hallway. Grandpa chatted about Danny fixing the barn, Danny planting a thousand walnut seedlings in the woods, Danny on the tractor mowing thistles, Danny drilling oat seed, Danny—

'Weren't you two going fishing?' Grandma asked.

Grandpa shrugged. 'We went this morning.'

Sara sat down next to Ben and reached for his hand under the table. Grandma served everybody. She didn't look like a ghost, nor did Grandpa. And Sara looked young again, early twenties. Her face had the full estrogen bloom of youth. Ben felt himself getting aroused pouring syrup on his grandma's pancakes, holding Sara's hand under the table, watching his grandpa gum his own syrup-soaked pancakes. Sara raised her eyebrows and winked. Ben blushed and pulled his hand away but Sara's fingers walked up the top of his thigh.

'Have you remembered yet where you put the fish?' Grandma asked.

'No, dear.'

'They aren't in the refrigerator or the freezer,' Grandma said.

'I put them down somewhere.' Grandpa looked very old now, near the end. Ben recognized that perhaps this was the day he would die.

'Don't worry.' Grandma stood behind him and kissed his bald spot. Then she said to Sara and Ben. 'Wait until you get old. Sometimes it feels as if you've forgotten your entire life.'

Ben could tell by his own hands and by the sound of his voice that he was young—but not too young. Sara Koepke's hand lingered on his thigh. He wanted it off but he also liked where it was. Was this their first time being so bold? Was this the start?

He asked to be excused. Grandma asked if he'd brought down his laundry.

'I'll get it,' he said. He wanted to look at Danny again at the top of the stairs. He'd convinced himself he must have invented what he saw, his brother's dead body turned into a giant fish.

'No, no, no,' his grandma said, stepping past him. 'You eat. I'll get the laundry.'

If she was a ghost, she looked very spry. Exceedingly healthy. And Grandpa looked exceedingly unhealthy. He began a coughing jag.

Grandma stepped into the living room and started up the stairs. Ben's heart leaped to his throat. She was going to see Danny the Fish! She was going to scream! He heard her footsteps pause at the landing.

'How sweet,' he heard her say.

Grandpa had stopped coughing. Now his face turned pale blue, and silent.

'My god, he's choking,' Sara said, suddenly standing.

Grandma wasn't screaming upstairs. She was laughing at the top of the stairs. Ben heard her feet on the steps coming down, pitter-patter.

'What a man,' she was saying. 'My husband.'

Grandpa was full blue now and Sara had positioned herself behind him, lifted him from his chair with her arms under his, gripped a fist against his sternum and jerked inward. Grandpa lunged forward and a piece of mushy pancakes-and-sausage flew out his mouth across the table and splatted against the red wallpaper. He took a huge breath just as a young Danny stepped through the back door into the kitchen and stood on the carpet of pink apple petals, holding a stringer of spotted brookies. He grinned and Grandpa yelled, 'My fish!' just as Grandma appeared from upstairs, holding up another stringer of pretty trout.

'Look what I found on the landing at the top of the stairs,' she said.

Everybody looked from Grandma with her fish to Danny with his and began to laugh. Everybody but Ben, who remembered now that this was the day. Even though his grandpa had been saved; even though Danny wasn't dead at the top of the stairs. Sara's face was smooth and her breasts firm and her waist narrow. It was spring and the creeks ran full and the sap flowed and his blood surged. He knew today was the day he'd betray his brother, and his grandfather was going to die.

But maybe he wasn't the only one to know it, because Grandpa's laugh quit first and his face took on a dazed expression. He put both elbows on the table and stared at the pancake stain on the red wallpaper as if it were art, or tea leaves at the bottom of a cup.

Then the scene froze, and turned granular, and became an old photograph, black-and-white, and what you could see in it was the future. Grandma looked at Grandpa with love and pity; and Ben looked with uncontrolled longing at Sara Koepke, standing at the sink now, her shoulders sloped forward and hands washing fish; and Danny, standing at the back door with apple petals strewn at his feet, careful and afraid, looked at Ben.

SOMETIME DURING THE NIGHT of his first day back home in twenty-five years, Ben woke from his frantic dreaming and wobbled dizzy to his bedroom window and took a deep breath. He hadn't actually even seen his brother yet—and felt relieved to have slept through his nap and what would have been an awkward dinner with Sara. But his dreams and memories had so buffeted him that he had to hold onto the sill to keep his balance. He felt suddenly sorry he'd come back to this place where it was so hard to control what he did and felt and thought—and life, it seemed, happened *to* him. *Your brother forgives you,* his mother's ghost had said. *Don't waste that.* Yet the one moral success of his life was managing to escape this farm—escape his out-of-control passion for his brother's girlfriend and then, the last year, his brother's wife. From the time Ben was nineteen until he was twenty-five they'd touched each other every chance they got—six years!—until he'd finally broken away in a last gasping effort to save himself.

And now he was back. Why? To what end? *We are in the middle,* Danny had written, *in the dark, and although I may have to lose everything eventually, I don't want to lose anything until I have to.*

Okay, Ben thought, whatever that means. But remembering Danny's words had calmed him, and he smelled the air, the great gulping fall chill, and he noticed in the moonlight yellow leaves drifting down from the birch trees along the driveway and swirling into the yard. He tried to recapture the euphoria he'd felt on the way home. The light of innocence, the airy possibility of redemption. Why not? He should have called ahead but he didn't and now here he was and he'd make the best of it. He'd wait for Danny to come home from wherever he was fishing this time. He lay down again in bed and felt the mattress warm against his body, the pillow slightly too large but good enough. He drifted back to sleep and woke up one more time before morning, felt the air in the room as cold as winter, his nose hairs freezing with each breath, snow swirling through the screen and piling on the inside sill. He shivered uncontrollably and remembered a nightmare he'd had as a boy of snow piling all the way up to the second story, and he and his mother standing at this very window, watching. He'd turned to his mother and asked what noise do ghosts make? And she duplicated the noise, a *boo-oo-oo-oo* from some deep and terrible place inside her. The frightening noise entered him and lifted him and held him, trembling, two feet off the ground before setting him down again—still trembling—at his mother's side.

Ben closed his eyes and hoped he'd never dream that dream again. It had been a long time. And his mother had been a good woman, never giving him cause to fear her. Out the window the wind blew hard. Something whooped in the yard, drifting up the hill like a lunatic bird. The air was cold but his head felt burning hot. He curled tighter into a ball and slept, and immediately dreamed he woke in a comfortable bed in a familiar room, a million dust motes sparkling in the yellow beam of sunshine that lit a stripe of his grandma's flowered wallpaper, and one sleeping black cat on the hardwood floor.

Black Bobbie, Ben thought, how odd—for she was a cat from his youth and had been dead for years.

He got up slowly, tiptoed to the window and saw the gabled barn roof over the garage. He looked below at the tipped-over Radio Flyer wagon on the green grass. He heard a thrush in the woods, a cardinal closer, and then he heard something behind him in the hallway. A muffled breathing, something moving on the carpet. He crept bravely to the door and cracked it, eyed the hallway, and there at the far end lay his brother and young Sara Koepke making love on the floor. She lay on her back, one bare leg straining upward as though trying to reach the ceiling, and the other draped over the wooded railing surrounding the stairwell.

'Shhhhh,' Sara said. 'Hear that?'

'No,' Danny said. He paused anyway. Ben couldn't see their heads, only their bodies, so they couldn't see him peeking through the crack in the door. Sara said, 'I think he's up,' and Danny said, 'I know I am!' And Sara whispered, 'Shhhhh, please,' and Danny began to move again. Sara's one leg straining upward had come down now and lay flat on the floor and she said, 'Hurry!'

Ben closed the door and remembered. In the mirror over the dresser he could see his smooth face, the chin hair of his mid-twenties, a tiny patch of chest hair on his sternum. The sounds of lovemaking continued in the hallway, and listening had given Ben a vicious desire to spill himself, his seed, or whatever he had inside him, to burst his pod and dissipate into the world. His blood, or Danny's. This was the day before the day he'd leave the farm for good. He put his hands over his ears. He closed his eyes and prayed that when he opened them again, he'd be someplace else but when he opened them, he was still in his room. He lifted both arms and flexed his biceps and his pectorals. He could feel a spring in his legs that he hadn't felt in a long time. He walked over to the window but by the time he got there he had to stand on tiptoe to see out. He pressed his nose against the screen, looked out at the pasture, white with snow. Something unpleasant had happened but he didn't know what. He couldn't remember what. He still had a sound in his head, though, and he put his hands back over his ears. The freezing air felt good on his face and in his lungs.

'Come here, boy.' It was Grandma and she gently removed his hands from his ears and lifted him onto her lap, held him tight against her chest.

'They've passed on,' she said.

'Where?'

Grandma didn't answer. Ben was afraid to look at her. He felt her quivering against his face.

'A better place,' she finally said. 'Where they wait for us.'

'They're waiting?'

'Yes, dear.'

'Grandma?'

'Yes?'

He smelled fish cooking. 'I can't remember their faces.'

'Oh, sweet,' she said, and held his head, hands on each side of his face. 'Sure you can. Think of them doing something. Think of something you saw them do often.'

Ben closed his eyes. He tried to see his mommy and daddy on the insides of his eyelids but couldn't. The fish smelled good and he was hungrier than he'd ever been in his life.

'Can you see them?'

'Yes,' he lied.

'To forget is to die,' she said. 'Don't ever forget.'

His mouth was watering against her chest. 'I'm hungry, Grandma.'

'We'll eat in just a minute,' she said, and still her chest quivered, his mouth watered, and so did her eyes.

'I can't wait,' he said.

'I'll tell you a story that might help.'

Ben opened his eyes. The snow was still falling outside the window, falling and falling and falling. He could look through the big window and see a trillion snowflakes in the narrow strip of sky between him and the wooded ridge.

'It had been days since Coyote had eaten,' Grandma said, 'and he saw a moose in the willows. He had no weapons, so he contorted his body, his face, and made the moose in the willows laugh so hard that it fell over and died.

'These animals are stupid, Coyote thought as he began to butcher the moose. He made a fire. And while the meat cooked, two trees began moaning above, the trunks rubbing together.

'*Stop that!* Coyote yelled. It sounded like lovemaking, and he was distracted.'

'What's lovemaking, Grandma?'

She smiled. 'Something very hard for Coyote to listen to, and he yelled *Stop!* but the wind did not stop, and the trees did not stop rubbing together and moaning. Poor Coyote! He was so distracted he climbed up one of the trees and tried to pull the branches apart. But he got stuck between the two rubbing branches and couldn't get loose. He struggled and struggled but couldn't get out.'

'Then what happened, Grandma?'

'Nothing,' she said, and touched each teary eye with her dress sleeve. 'He stayed stuck. And he had to watch two wolves come by and eat his food.'

'Silly Coyote,' Ben said.

'Yes,' Grandma said.

'Does Danny know that story?'

'I don't know,' Grandma said.

'Where is Danny?'

'He's feeding cows.'

'By himself?'

'With Grandpa,' she said.

'Let's tell him the story when he comes in.'

Her eyes were dry now. 'Okay, let's.'

'And then we can eat?'

'Yes,' she said.

BEN STOOD AT THE TOP of the stairs, his dead-brother-turned-fish at his feet. Sara stepped backward down the stairs and hooked her hands under Danny's gills and began to pull.

'Lift his tail around,' she said. 'Then push.'

Ben did and the big fish began sliding headfirst down the stairs. Slowly at first and then faster. Too fast. The tail slipped out of his hands.

'Christ!' Sara said, squealing with delight as she turned to run ahead of the sliding fish to get out of the way. Danny the Fish made it most of the way to the bottom of the stairs but couldn't turn the corner and slide the last three steps into the living room. He bumped his snout against the plaster wall and wedged himself into the corner.

Sara repositioned herself from below, re-grabbed Danny's gills and began to turn him. Ben felt helpless. He couldn't get a good grip on Danny's slippery tail. He stood higher up the stairs and watched her wrestle the big head around the ninety-degree corner and partway through the doorway into the living room. She pulled, and Danny slid. She pulled again, and Danny got stuck between the doorjambs. Ben tried to help by pushing, but Danny's tail was too limp.

'Step over him,' she said.

Ben tried, but Danny was too big. He tried again, stretching his stride in an awkward way to get over Danny's fish body jammed in the doorway. Still he couldn't. So he just put his foot on Danny's side and Danny made a sound like a burp as Ben stepped over him into the living room with Sara.

The two of them grabbed Danny's gill vents and pulled, and Danny came sliding out onto the hardwood floor, minus some scales that remained stuck to the doorjamb.

'Good god,' Ben said. He picked up the cluster of scales. It was the size of his palm. He held it in one hand, then the other, and then set it down on the floor. He noticed the dorsal fin had partly detached, too, and he tried to re-position it along Danny's back.

'Look what we've done,' he said.

Sara Koepke ran into the kitchen and came back with a tube of superglue. She squatted next to Danny and carefully, lovingly, Ben thought, reattached the dorsal fin.

'There,' she said.

She put the tube of glue in the right front pocket of her cutoff shorts. Ben couldn't help but admire her legs, still lovely after these many years. She noticed him looking but her brow furrowed, all business. 'Let's pull him out the front door onto the lawn.'

They carefully turned him upright so he'd fit through the door, and pulled him out onto the stoop. He slid like a seal down the concrete steps and into the grass. It was hot and humid; a haze hung over the hollow. Ben felt his pores prick open and immediately he was wet with sweat.

'Get the hose,' Sara said. 'I'll get the wagon.'

Ben walked around the side of the house and picked up the green hose. He turned on the faucet and felt the hose sputter and snort, and by the time he got back to Danny again the water was flowing in a clear stream. He let it splash and wash the length of Danny from his tail to his head and back again. Then he set the hose down and hefted Danny over to rinse his other side. Next he took a long drink himself, and even held the hose above his head. The cold water took his breath away. He stood up and shook his wet hair, wiped his eyes and face with the back of his forearm and saw Sara emerge from the side yard pulling the red Radio Flyer wagon. The two of them lifted Danny up onto it. First his head, and then his tail, both of which flopped well over the edges. In fact they had to make a slight adjustment so his tail wouldn't drag on the ground, and then Ben sprayed Danny with the hose again. Sara picked up the handle and began pulling the wagon across the lawn and onto the gravel driveway.

'Where are we taking him?' Ben asked.

'His favorite place in the world,' she said.

Ben followed behind Sara as she pulled the wagon down the long driveway, over the bridge spanning the Rio Benji (a creek, really, three feet across) up through the hayfield to the county road, then left toward the big river, Old Danny River. The same way they'd ridden their bikes just this morning . . . or was that years ago?

Ben listened to the birds in the trees to the right of the road and to the regular squeak of the wagon wheels and to the plastic tires on the road. Ahead the heat rose in waves off the blacktop.

'Wait,' he said, as he felt himself suddenly struggling to keep up. His legs so tired, his side aching . . . He shouted '*Wait!*' again, in a high, piercing voice. '*Waaaaaait!*'

Sara Koepke slowed briefly but didn't stop pulling the wagon. She wore blue pedal pushers, a peach tank top, and her face was freckled and smooth. Instead of a giant fish, a turtle the size of a cowboy hat lay rolled over on its shell in the wagon.

'Where's Danny?' Ben asked.

'Up there,' she said, and pointed.

Sure enough, Danny as a boy was running toward the house in the pasture carrying a fish like a football. Ben could see the soles of his sneakers as he ran away, and he could see a fish tail flapping this way and that under his arm.

Sara turned around after him and now pulled the wagon back toward the house. 'Hurry,' she said when she passed him. Ben tried to follow but his side ached terribly when he ran and he had to slow down and then stop.

'We'll be in the bathroom!' Sara shouted back to him.

Grandpa was working in the shadowy garage and called out a greeting through the big open door. The red Radio Flyer was parked empty behind the house, by the back door, and Ben went in that way. He tiptoed through the kitchen and spotted his grandma asleep on the couch in the living room. The water ran in the bathroom and the door stood open. He went in. Danny and Sara stood looking into the rapidly filling tub where the bass lay floating on its side and the turtle walked in place, trying to get out, its feet gaining no tread on the smooth white bathtub surface.

Danny turned the water off, disappointed that the fish hadn't survived. Ben and Sara followed him out of the bathroom, across the kitchen and then out again into the yard.

'Maybe if we fill the wagon with water,' Danny said, 'we can get a fish back alive.'

'Maybe,' Sara Koepke said.

Ben couldn't believe they were going to walk all the way to the ponds again. He didn't think he could do it but didn't see how he could stay behind.

Then, from the bathroom window, and from every other open window in the house, came Grandma's scream: '*Get these animals out of my bathroom!*'

OH, WHAT A STRANGE trip home! Would there be no waking relief? No solid ground to stand on? How was anything real to happen if Ben could never escape the dreams and memories and stories that lived and breathed here? How was he to forgive himself and find a place in his heart again for brotherly love? He'd flown home on a jet plane. He'd driven a rental car from the airport. He'd walked in the door of the farmhouse and up the stairs with Sara Koepke and sat feverish on his bed and told her he was tired and needed to sleep. She'd touched him and his blood rushed to his skin and he shivered. Then he'd slept and dreamed. Dreamed visions and voices. Dreamed heat and cold, waking and walking. Or remembered. The memories and dreams crowding out the here and now. Hadn't he suspected it would be this way?

He gasped for breath in bed, began to sweat and pray but was interrupted by footsteps on the wood floor of his room. He blinked and stared but couldn't see anything. He pulled the covers around himself and shivered. Why such an icy chill? The shadow came closer and he felt the weight of a cold hand on his shoulder. Whose hand? The sheets pulled back and the hand slid from his shoulder down to his hand.

'Who are you?' he asked, or tried to ask, but even before he formed the question he knew.

'Come,' Grandma said.

'Where are we going?' he asked, but she didn't speak, only turned to walk ahead of him, her white nightgown flowing now, long and flowing and billowing—was she there at all? He followed her in his plaid boxer shorts through the bedroom door and across the carpet to the landing. No body, no smell of death, or fish on a stringer. Still he stepped lightly and quickly, and then down the stairs into the dark living room, through the kitchen and pantry toward the back door. He felt the weight of his penis still heavy with blood and he felt afraid his grandma would turn around and notice, but she only pulled open the back door and pushed open the screen, and they stepped out into the perfumed night. He didn't feel cold anymore.

'Where are we going?' he asked again.

'I've been watching your confused nonsense,' she said, 'and there are spirits you need to know.'

Across the pasture he could see a herd of horses standing still as statues, their silhouettes lit by a crescent moon rising through the trees behind them. The grass was wet with dew. Ben shivered. Grandma led the way up the ridge road and into the woods, through thick brush toward the orchard. She ate blackberries she picked in the woods and venison pemmican from her pocket. She paused in her eating to point to the ruins of a log homestead on the site of an Indian ghost village, later to become a station on the Underground Railroad, past a rock wall against which Union troops had shot several hundred Rebel prisoners.

Ben didn't see any of these things. Only dripping forest and drying milkweed and Queen Anne's lace. He thought perhaps his grandma was crazy and mentioned it to her. She shrugged and said, 'We are never so alone as when we can no longer feel the dead.'

In the orchard clearing, he shivered. She moved over next to him and he liked the warmth of her body.

'Pay attention,' she said.

'To what?'

'To that.'

Below them in the valley a trail of stragglers stretched like a line of ants eastward all the way to the horizon.

'They're walking across the continent,' Grandma said.

'Why?'

'They have nowhere else to go.'

'Why?'

'Don't they look terrible?'

Ben had to admit they did. Dressed in rags, their faces ravaged by sun and pinched with hunger.

'Many are sick with grief,' she said. 'Or with cholera, scurvy, dysentery, exhaustion, disillusionment. They will arrive at their frontier destination brutalized and hurting, often in need of non-existent professional help.'

'Who are they?' Ben asked.

'Haven't you ever heard of the pioneers?'

Some of the figures were clear to Ben, and others less so. Sometimes they faded as if to vapor and all he could see was the gray valley, the colorless grass, and the black oak and hickory skeletons leafless on the hillsides.

'Look!'

An old man sat leaning against a tree.

'Who's he?'

Grandma shrugged. 'He's sick with malaria and has asked to be dumped from the family wagon to die beside the trail.'

'And that one?'

Ben pointed at another man, eyes black wild, sweat shining on his brow as he knelt in the grass and hammered his tools to useless scrap.

'Why is he doing that?'

Grandma took another bite of pemmican and offered some to Ben, who refused.

'His mule died so he can't carry the tools any farther, and he'll be damned if anybody else is going to use them.'

'And those people?' Ben said, pointing. 'What's that smoke?'

'That group has lost all its oxen. They are burning the pasture so the next group of emigrants has no grass for their surviving beasts.'

'Why are you showing me this?' Ben asked.

'I'm not showing you anything. You're seeing.'

"I don't understand.'

'Some found gold,' she said. 'Others found deep soil and the corn grew high, leaves rattling in the wind. But the soil was soaked with native blood, as was the gold. None of it was free, not ever. And in bad years there was more than enough suffering to go around. Drought withered the crops and turned the grass brown so it crackled under bare feet, and the grasshoppers flew in and ate everything that was left, even the paint off the barns. Children died of snake bites and whooping cough, diphtheria, spinal fever, brain fever, measles, typhoid, pneumonia, and storms blew barns down in a clap of dry oak planks, a finger of tornado dipping like the finger of God himself, or a squadron of bombers, and the blizzards, too, like the one that blew your great-grandmother away.'

'What?'

'You've forgotten everything, haven't you?'

Ben shook his head. He wished he were back at work in our nation's capital, back in the lab where his world was black-and-white, he wore the right clothes and ate at the right places for lunch, and where those around him would never talk to him like this.

'Your great-grandfather Clarence, the lipless old man who slept under the Indian scalp blanket, lost his first wife to diphtheria, her and their two children. And after a decade of savage grief and brutality, he remarried a young woman whom he truly loved. He settled down. They started dairying. It was early winter and they'd been out in the barn doing evening chores when a hard wind began to blow from the north. Frigid, arctic wind, and suddenly the driveway turned to ice so slippery they couldn't walk the slight grade back to the house. So they had to crawl to move, to gain any traction, and maybe the distance on all fours would take, what, three minutes most? Well, sometime during that little trek the snow came and the wind blew harder and they couldn't see a foot in front of their faces. A white blackness descended from the sky and Clarence led the way straight into it. He felt his bride's hand on his ankle and then he didn't anymore. She'd blown away, blown backward, and he tried frantically to find her but the big wind had caught her skirt and coat and she sailed backward on the ice, disappeared into the night and cold, swallowed by the wind like his voice when he called after her. For three days the wind blew and Clarence tried desperately to find her. He left a crying child, your grandpa, in the house and tied himself to the porch with a long rope and made forays out into the visionless, deep freeze, the belly of the blizzard.

'Then the wind stopped. The morning dawned clear and cold, and the sky a fragile eggshell blue.'

'Did he find her?'

Grandma nodded. 'Froze to a tree almost a mile from the house, the only tree between them and the river, so if the wind hadn't bumped her against that tree, she might have blown away forever, and what a thing to happen to a man, his first wife and children die from unseen bugs that cause a fever that steams the brain, and his second wife is carried off by a cold wind. No wonder he slaughtered Indians.'

Ben felt depressed. A headache racked his brain. 'I've never heard so many awful stories,' he said.

'Oh, wake up,' she said, and winked. 'That's only your grandpa's side of the family, so you've already forgotten mine. Where do you think all those bones in the pasture come from? Do you think any of your ancestors have made it through here without dying?'

'Enough!' He put his hands over his ears and closed his eyes. 'I can't stand it!'

'Sure you can,' she said, and led him out of the orchard and down out of the woods and into the valley shrouded suddenly by night. She led him by his hand toward where the horses stood still as statues.

'Where are we going, Grandma?'

'To a place,' she said, 'where you may see visions and dream hard dreams, where your heart might open again to the big world itself, or at least to your own sorrow and joy.'

'I don't understand,' Ben said.

'I know you don't,' she said, 'so pay attention or you'll lose your mind. Hell, you might lose it anyway.'

They approached a barbed wire fence and Grandma passed through it without climbing it.

'How did you do that?' he asked her.

'Practice,' she said.

Confused, Ben said, 'You opened the door of the house, didn't you? How come you can pass through the fence, but you had to open the door?'

'I opened the door for you,' she said, and turned to hold down the top wire so he could carefully step over.

'There,' she said. 'Now let me pick berries for the journey.'

Ben couldn't see any berries, or bushes for that matter. They were standing in the middle of an empty pasture, silver with moonlight, and Grandma bent down and reached, and pretended to pick and pretended to eat.

'Mmmm,' she said.

Ben did exactly as she did, pretending to pick, putting his hand to his mouth as she did and mysteriously tasting the tart earth flavor of blackcaps.

'It's a miracle,' he said.

Grandma laughed. 'Eat all you can now,' she said. 'You're going on a long journey and you can't eat again until we get home.'

He ate until his stomach was full and then his grandma took his hand and led him into the forest. 'This way,' she said, and they walked for a long time. Because there was no familiar landmark to walk toward or away from, Ben got confused and thought they may have circled around and crossed the same creek twice. Which was okay, because they walked all night and by the next day the sun was hot and each time he crossed the creek he got down on his hands and knees and drank deeply. He guessed by the color and ripeness of the grasses that it was midsummer in the afternoon, but by evening the sky grayed and he felt a fall chill, then at night the cold descended from the starry heavens. The frozen ground squeaked under his step. His hands and ears grew numb. He felt his pockets for matches but found none. He passed leafless trees with black branches, approached a band of gypsies dancing around a fire, begged a blanket, and continued walking. He passed a Cornish family looking for lead to mine, passed Norwegians and Irish looking for lost relatives. He wandered through a village of Swiss immigrants, sleeping quietly, cheese on their breath. He'd lost track of his grandma a long time ago but didn't even care. He was so cold, so cold. He wrapped himself in the blanket and passed a Bavarian tavern crowded with drunken singers; he spoke briefly with a group of Lycra-clad cyclists looking for a marked campsite.

'There's a historical place around here somewhere,' one of them said. 'Do you know where?'

Ben didn't. He passed a family of immigrants just off a river boat, carpet bags in their hands, faces stunned.

'So this is America,' one of them said in Polish. 'Everyone's mad!'

The sky began to gray with morning and on the horizon for many miles hung a line of smoke, announcing to the natives far and wide that civilization was dawning.

Ben watched a retreating column of Indians, shoeless on the frozen ground, blankets torn and buffalo robes. They passed silently, the old and the young and the broken, all of them starving and slinking toward the forest.

'Where are you going?' Ben asked.

'Walleye Lake,' one of them answered.

Another said cheerfully, 'We can spear fish there!'

Ben watched the column disappear into the dark, and he felt the cold wind, and he felt hungry and cold and alone and he didn't know where he was or where to go, or what to do. Suddenly he heard his grandma's voice. 'This way,' she said, her mouth full of something. He heard her chewing.

'What are you eating, Grandma?'

'None of your beeswax,' she said, and laughed. Her hand found his shoulder, his arm, his hand. 'Come.'

As they walked the rest of the night his grandma ate an entire ham, a chicken, and a tube of potato chips. The smell of the food, the sound of the chewing caused Ben great suffering, but she said it was for his own good. It was what fasting was about, suffering. They paused for a night in a cave on a bluff above the river. It was a place he knew, but he couldn't remember how.

'Rest here,' Grandma said, and sat down. He sat next to her and was about to ask her something but she held up her hand. 'Don't speak,' she said. 'Your voice hasn't changed and it may scare the spirits.'

'What spirits?'

'Never mind.' She wiped her mouth with her sleeve. 'Just sit here and catch your breath and wait for a moment until your eyes adjust.'

Ben stood blinking, holding her big rough hand.

'See the bones in back?' she asked, her mouth full, her breath like mustard and ham.

'No,' he said.

'Well, see the people clustered over there?'

'I don't see anything, Grandma.'

'Watch.'

'I can't see anything.'

'Quiet,' she said. 'If they hear your voice, they will disappear.'

'Who?' Ben asked.

'My people,' she said. 'Yours. Now hush and stop shaking. Shadow is your friend. Without him you're flat as paper. Are you cold?'

'Yes,' Ben whispered.

'Then let's climb on the pile to stay warm.'

'What pile?' But she'd led him there, and Ben felt all of the warm limbs, the bodies woven together like a pile of puppies.

'Their men are away and they are huddled together, afraid of the white men with guns.'

He lay down on top of the pile of people, squeezed down for warmth.

'Grandma?' Ben whispered, but she didn't answer. More bodies pressed against him, so heavy he feared he couldn't breathe. But he could. Sure. Steady, steady, he felt safe again, and he slept, and in the morning somebody stood looking down at him in the bed.

'Why aren't you up already?'

'Me?'

It was Grandpa. 'Come on, kiddo. You want to be a bum like me? Time to get dressed for school.'

Grandpa grabbed his covers and pulled them off and laughed heartily. Ben had a clean white cast on his leg. 'Here, I'll help you up, boy. This is golden America. You can be what you like, but you have to go to school!'

'Where's Mom?'

'What?' Grandpa's face went pale. Then Grandma's face over Grandpa's shoulder, her lively black eyes and careful mouth, and lips that made him stare.

'We're going to take care of you now,' she said.

'Why?' Ben asked. The cast on his leg was heavy and he felt a dull ache in his shin bone. When he was sleeping he'd forgotten that he had a broken leg. Forgotten about the hospital and the new cast. He also felt guilty for something else he'd forgotten.

Grandpa looked at Grandma and whispered, 'Haven't you told him?'

'Of course I did!' she whispered back. 'But he doesn't seem to want to understand.'

She took Ben up in her arms. His cast made his leg hang down low. He smelled the skin of Grandma's neck as he peeked over her shoulder at the rug at the top of the stairs. Blue and pink, with a green water stain the shape of a large fish.

'Oh my god he's got a fever,' Grandma said. 'He's burning up!' She turned around and lay him back down on the bed and covered him against the cold.

'And Danny?'

'Downstairs eating his Cocoa Puffs,' Grandma said. 'Tomorrow when you're better there'll be a bowl for you, too. And then it'll be off to school for you brave warriors.'

THE BLACKTOP ROAD STRAIGHTENED on the flood plain and distant bluffs rose hazy though the sultry air. Sara Koepke was pulling the wagon. Most of the water had spilled from the edges and Danny the Giant Bass had dried out in the sun. Flies gathered on his eyes. Ben waved them off. The smell was strong in the heat.

'What about the girls?' Ben asked.

'Are you trying to be funny?' she asked.

'No,' Ben said. He stepped faster to catch up with her, to walk next to her.

'What do you expect me to tell them?' Sara said.

'Tell them that their father is dead,' he said.

The exertion of the walk had formed a sheen of perspiration on her forehead and upper lip. Without looking at him, she said, 'Do you think that's something they'd really like to know?'

Ben tried to remember hearing about his parents' death but couldn't. He'd been too small, too young. 'They'll find out soon enough,' he said. 'Next time they come to visit.'

'Well, that's when I'll tell them,' she said.

They walked a while longer. Sara seemed to accelerate every time Ben stepped up to walk next to her, so he let himself fall back a step and she kept the pace steady. The road crossed a wide plain, and the sun burned down on them, and when they approached a tree, they took a break. Sara pulled the wagon into the spot of shade next to the trunk, but there wasn't enough room for both of them and the wagon, so she pushed the wagon back out into the sunshine again. The heat and dryness had paled Danny's color, and a cluster of flies crawled on his head and in his mouth. Ben waved his hand at the flies and they scattered, but as soon as he stopped they gathered again.

'Oh, christ,' Sara said, and looked away.

Ben sat down next to her with his back to the trunk of the tree. They didn't look at each other. They looked at each other's legs stretching out in the grass. Hers were bare, and even with the smell of his dead brother, even with the flies and the sweat and the heat, Ben was seized by a desire to make love to her. He wondered if she might have the same idea, so he glanced at the side of her face but she was looking at Danny the Fish in the too-bright sun, and he couldn't tell what she was thinking and felt suddenly awkward and uncertain. He closed his eyes and tried to remember his life in our nation's capital. Tried to remember his home, the stoop, the painted brick, the Asian restaurants on the corner, the coffee shop, the neighbors of color—how did they live, he wondered? Tears filled his eyes. He loved his life in our nation's capital. On a morning like this he'd be reading the paper, eating a melon. Life was good and wasn't that normal? In the street, if he looked out his front window, nobody would be dragging around a dead brother transformed into a fish, nor accusing anybody else of anything unpleasant, at least not at this hour, on this day, in his neighborhood. All of his friends were from other places, and they'd come to the capital for the good work. They had beautiful homes and healthy hobbies. They traveled. They trained for triathlons. They studied Spanish.

Why would he ever leave such a place?

He opened his eyes again and Sara Koepke had moved very close to him. She gave him an odd but compelling look and kissed him on the mouth. He tasted something bitter on her tongue and liked it. He greedily held her face to his and enthusiastically tasted more of her. She had to use both hands to push him away long enough to take a breath and say, 'I'm sorry.'

'What?'

She nodded toward Danny's fish eye peering over the edge of the red wagon. 'Not with him watching, okay?'

ON THE WAY BACK FROM THE CAVE, Grandma told Ben that his great-grandfather Clarence—his grandfather's father—had been one of the white men with guns who had chased the Indian women and children into the cave. He'd been one of the men that her people—including her own mother as a little girl—had been hiding from.

Ben felt bad but didn't know what to say.

His grandma touched his shoulder with her big, rough hand. 'Don't worry if you don't know what to say,' she said. 'It's not about talking anyway. It's not even about *thinking*. It's about doing. *Loving*, I should say. Loving something or someone. And *feeling* it. The whole mess of it. The beautiful—my mother told me she escaped on the back of a raven!—*and* the ugly. Try to hold all of that in your heart and only then should you think. Only then do you have anything to say.'

Ben could feel his middle-age body struggling to keep up with his grandma. 'I'm fifty years old,' he said. 'Haven't I done a lot? Lived a lot?'

'You've forgotten everything,' she said.

'I came home,' he said.

'You did,' she said. 'You went away years ago and had your brain vacuumed out so you could feel clean and innocent and you thought all of this would be easy. You came home dumb.'

Ben wanted to argue but stopped himself. What did it matter what she said anyway? What was he going to do, get into an argument with his dead grandma in a dream? They were walking across a dark pasture and then under big crooked pin oaks along the edge of a woodlot.

'It's my fault,' she said. 'I should have done this earlier.'

'Done what?'

'No man is prepared or fitted to begin his true life until he has fasted and accomplished his great journey,' she said, and took his hand and they dropped down from the edge of the woodlot toward the middle of a meadow.

'I don't understand, Grandma.'

'Then listen,' she said. 'Here's a start. Your true love is in there.' She pointed and Ben looked at the empty gray field before him, at the silver sky growing on the horizon.

'In where?' he said.

'That lodge. See the one small window glowing yellow from a light within? See the smoke rising from the chimney and spreading low in the sky?'

Ben didn't but was afraid to say so.

'Where's the door?' he said.

'Around back.'

She led him in a circle through the tall grass. She stopped and pointed again. Ben stepped away from her and pretended to open a door. He heard it creak. He stepped inside, where the air was warmer and smelled of sweat and smoke and coffee. He stood still for a moment, but still could see nothing except the prairie growing gradually lighter around him. Grandma disappeared, and for a moment he panicked, thinking he was alone, but then he sensed the presence of a moving shadow near him.

'Who are you?'

No answer, but the ghost began to prepare something to eat.

Here, it said, handing Ben an invisible plate.

'I don't think I'm supposed to eat anything,' Ben said.

The ghost shrugged and took the plate back. The sun appeared like a red ball on the horizon and birds began to sing the new day.

You wait here, the ghost said. *I'll be back.*

Ben looked around at the tall grass sparkling with dew. 'Where is *here*?' he asked.

Here night is day, and day is night.

'What's that supposed to mean?'

It means, the ghost explained, *that when the sun goes down again there will be more activity.*

'Oh.' Ben was going to ask what kind of activity but the ghost had disappeared into a long shadow.

It was a slow day waiting. To pass the time, he thought of his days in our nation's capital, how at noon he'd leave his office cubicle, pass through the maze of other cubicles, then take a stairway down into the giant factory, where he followed the painted yellow line on the floor into a tunnel that led to a carpeted locker room, where he received his laundered clothes from the lovely and talented towel girl, changed, and descended a well-lighted metal stairway to the racquetball courts. He loved the light and smell of the racquetball courts. He loved the endless geometry of the game. He carefully remembered tournaments he'd played, the details of long and vigorous games he had won, and of games he should have won.

The sun climbed higher. He felt terribly hungry. Also hot and thirsty. But he forced himself to stay put because the ghost had instructed him to, and also because his grandma had told him that fasting would bring him clarity—and at his age, how could he not want a little clarity? And if that wasn't motive enough, his grandma had told him his true love was here. He'd been lonely for a long time and it would be a good thing to be able to visit the farm without coveting his brother's wife. So he cast about in his memory for more things to keep his mind occupied while he waited. He mentally recited the batting order of World Series championship baseball teams going back twenty years. He named an All-World Series team for those same twenty years, and argued with himself about certain key positions. He calculated how many home runs X would have to average for the next twelve years to beat Y's career home run total.

Then, for a change, and because he wondered which he might see tonight, he imagined all of his ex-lovers standing in a line, long but not too terribly long, and he moved from one woman to the next, conjuring appealing details about each and every one.

Their smells, their smiles, their eyes. Their anger. Their gentleness. The sound of their voices.

But none of them stood out as the love of his life, so he divided them into two groups, the Gliders and the Others. Gliders moved as fish did swimming, as birds flying. They moved so smoothly and effortlessly in sex that when he was with them his own body seemed to disappear, to become weightless.

The Others were the others. They were learning, or would never learn, or were having a bad day. But individually they were easier to remember than the Gliders, and more interesting, too, because their hitches and difficulties made them unique and provided windows into their solitude through which, even from this distance, he could look and wonder.

When the sun finally set on the prairie, Ben heard men's voices faintly talking around him. By the light of a small fire, he could see he was sitting at one end of a long house, at a long table with many other vague forms, shadows. He recognized some of them. His parents and his grandma and grandpa, and beyond them the shadowy figure of his Great-grandfather Clarence with his lipless smile. Closer, Ben could see his brother Danny, who looked happy—although his face was pale and when Ben reached for him, his skin was ice cold. A spirit (the one who had tried to feed him the morning before) whispered to Ben that he was in the lodge of the dead and he could pick anybody he liked to pull back into the world of the living. He only had to choose. His mother or father, his grandpa or grandma, great-grandfather, or his brother—

Then suddenly he saw Sara Koepke. Had she died? Or was she just a visitor like him? Maybe she was faking it.

'She's not dead,' he said to the spirit.

To you she is.

As transparent as she was, she still looked young and pretty. When she smiled at him, she looked so alive that it was easy to choose her—he couldn't help himself! He felt guilty about it even as he pointed to her and took her hand and guided her out of the lodge and into the tall grass, the love of his life, his brother's wife.

Ashamed for his choice, for leaving dead family members and taking Sara Koepke, Ben dropped her hand and turned to walk away. The lodge of the dead disappeared behind him. He could hear Sara move through the grass next to him but he felt too terrible even to glance at her. From somewhere above, the spirit whispered that he was not to touch her again during their long journey home, which Ben didn't figure to be hard because when he felt brave enough to look again she was still mostly transparent.

Nevertheless, as the hours progressed, he could see her more and more clearly. They camped at daybreak, and walked the next night and camped again, and on the third dawn, when they stopped to rest and he made a fire and the light played on her face and he could see the sheen of her skin, and her tongue between her lips, he could not resist the joyous impulse that overtook him. He jumped up and ran around the fire to embrace her.

'*Stop!*' she screamed.

But it was too late. Just as he touched her, she vanished and the campfire went out. Ben found himself alone and very hungry in the dark. He shivered. Above him two trees moaned in the wind where their trunks rubbed together. They sounded as if they were making love.

'Stop!' he yelled, but they didn't stop.

He wept through the day and into the night. His sorrow was as deep as anything he'd ever felt. The sun came up on a new day, and his hunger had dulled and he felt listless and fatigued. He squatted in the pasture and shit, then asked his shit what in the world he should do but he heard no answer. Was he going crazy? Perhaps. For some reason the notion didn't even scare him. He heard a mourning dove coo and he shivered and decided to walk home. He walked all day, stumbling left foot in front of right, and as he walked the last half mile down the valley past the ponds, dusk settled and then darkness fell. Only the hanging sky, lit marvelously with stars, gave shape to the wooded hills, to the barn, and to the erect house planted firmly at the end of the hollow.

He entered through the back door, tiptoed through the kitchen in the dark, then up the stairs, where he turned the corner at the landing and ran smack into his living brother in the dark. They bumped heads.

'Jesus!' Danny's voice. 'I thought you *saw* me!'

Ben—disconcerted, scared—said, 'I thought you were coming home tomorrow.'

Danny stood rubbing his forehead with his big fist, his yellow-gray hair a tangle. He held a hammer in his left hand that he seemed to have forgotten about. 'It *is* tomorrow,' he said. He grinned and looked at his watch. 'Well, just barely.'

Ben put his hand on the wall for balance.

'You all right? You look pale.'

Ben looked down at himself. Had he been sleepwalking? He was wearing only his plaid boxer shorts. 'I'm fine. It's nice to see you.'

'Same here, Benji. Where you been?'

Ben didn't know how to explain that he didn't know where he'd been. Wandering around somewhere in his underwear? In a dream where he'd just betrayed his brother again, where he'd happily taken Sara out of the lodge of the dead instead of him.

'I guess I went for a walk,' he said, 'I guess I couldn't sleep.'

Danny touched Ben's shoulder and the skin around his eyes wrinkled into a smile. 'Checking out the place in the middle of the night?'

Ben shrugged.

'How does it feel?'

Ben didn't know how to say all he'd felt since he'd been home. 'I've been a little feverish, I think. I can't believe I'm back.'

Danny nodded and looked at the floor. 'When Sara called me and said you were here I drove home as fast as I could.'

'I'm glad,' Ben said, and he suddenly was. To stand here in this hallway with his living brother. To look at his brother's kind face.

Danny lifted the hammer and gently tapped the plaster.

'What you doing?'

'Dead rat behind this wall.'

Ben sniffed, nodded, and Danny laughed, newly animated. 'Last week I took the cover off the light socket and dumped a little poison back there. Thought he'd start to die and head out for some water, but he must have got stuck. Hey, you sure you're all right?'

Again Ben had put the flat of his hand on the wall to keep from falling over. 'I guess I'm hungry,' he said. 'I'm starved.'

Danny smiled, green eyes delighted. 'There's chicken in the fridge,' he said. 'Help yourself.'

But when Ben went downstairs and tried to eat, the dead rodent smell had spread into the kitchen and when he opened the fridge, it seemed to get even worse. The chicken was cold and looked under-cooked and that, along with the bad smell and new guilt, took away his appetite. He poured himself a tall glass of whiskey and sat in the dark and listened to his brother puttering in the hallway, tapping on the plaster with the hammer as though to hear where the rat's body lay decaying. Then the tapping stopped and the stairwell light switched off. Before he went to bed, Danny came down and stood in the entry between the kitchen and the living room and said, 'I can't believe you're here, Benji. I'm very happy to see you.'

'Me too,' Ben said, and lifted his glass. 'Finally.'

'Thanks for coming.'

'It's been a little confusing,' Ben said, and as he said so, he tried to reassure himself that in *real life*, as opposed to a sleepwalking *dream*, he'd have chosen to take his brother out of the lodge of the dead—wouldn't he?

'I keep seeing Grandma.'

'Yeah?' Danny said.

'And Grandpa. It's like they're ghosts. Or memories. I don't know which.'

Danny shrugged. 'I don't believe in ghosts,' he said, 'but I know what you mean. I remember them so vividly it's as if they never left.'

Ben raised his glass. 'Join me?'

Danny shook his head and said it'd been too long of a day already and he had to go to sleep. Would Ben forgive him if he went to bed?

'Of course,' Ben said. 'Tomorrow, then.'

'Tomorrow and tomorrow,' his brother said.

'I'll save you some.'

Danny smiled again. 'Or drink it all and we'll buy some more.' Then he turned and crossed the living room into his and Sara's bedroom. Ben sat still for just a moment and listened to the sounds of the old house creaking in a big wind. He tried to remember what he'd done with the day. He remembered waking up to an empty house. He napped and woke up. After how long, he wasn't quite sure anymore. He'd taken a walk to the ponds? No, that must have been years ago. Mainly what he'd done since he got home is sleep. He'd woken at least once to look out the window, he remembered that. And then obviously he'd taken a walk in his sleep. He must have. How else had he ended up in the hallway in his underwear, bumping into his brother? What a way to come home! He thought of his grandma and grandpa still here. He wouldn't tell Danny about their mother the ghost—but he did want to ask what Danny remembered about her and their dad. Ben remembered their deaths more than he remembered them, but Danny would have been nine when they died and would remember more. He finished the whiskey, set the tumbler on the counter, and climbed the stairs to his boyhood bedroom and climbed into bed. His sheets felt cold and damp, and Ben had the uncanny feeling that Sara had been there waiting for him until she couldn't any longer, until she had to get up and leave.

But no, he thought, as he curled up into his own heat again. That was a long time ago, as was everything else that had been passing through his mind during this strange trip home. He heard the wind in the cedar tree outside the window, the wind rattle the metal stove chimney, the wind bang the basement door, the wind send an empty can rattling across the gravel driveway. *A long time ago*, he thought again, and immediately fell into a deep sleep.

HE WOKE IN THE GRASS on the side of the river road, his head in Sara Koepke's lap. Around him lay the old familiar hills under a cobalt blue sky.

'I finally saw Danny,' he said.

Sara smiled tenderly. 'He's changed.'

Ben sat up and looked at the Red Flyer the wagon. Danny had a big round belly and a wide scythe tail that flopped over the rim of the wagon almost to the ground. He'd changed from a giant bass into a tuna.

'He was a man,' Ben said. 'He wasn't a fish.'

Sara lifted her hands to her face and sniffed, then wrinkled her nose.

'When we get to the river we can swim and clean up a little, but according to the data I got from the computer, we have to take him to the ocean now.'

'What?'

'Remember the X'tilc' people of Zo?' she asked.

'No,' he said.

'Don't be that way. He was your brother.'

Ben felt suddenly sheepish. He remembered bumping heads with Danny in the dark at the top of the stairs, but certainly that couldn't have killed him. He remembered the gladness he felt standing in the hallway with him. Sitting down in the kitchen with him. The glass of whiskey in his own hand. That was real, wasn't it? He wanted to get back there.

'I want to wake up,' Ben said. 'I want to go home.'

'Well, according to the website,' Sara instructed, 'the species of the fish has to be determined. Then the fish is transported to a body of water that contains that species. Remember now?'

Ben didn't, but he nodded anyway. What was the use of trying to figure anything out? Was anything ever clearer than the simple feel of the hot sun hot on his back, on his bare legs, the top of his head? He stood up over the fish and studied its new blue sheen, perfect curves. Its big body over-filled the wagon and a cluster of flies swarmed its gold eyes and open mouth. Ben waved them away.

'Which way?' he asked.

'Eventually all roads lead to the same place.'

'Christ,' Ben said.

'Trust me.'

Ben picked up the wagon handle and began to pull his brother along the road behind her. It wasn't so much that he trusted her sense of direction, but that the road ahead followed a familiar rail fence northward down the valley toward the river. The wagon squeaked and rattled over every rut, but Ben held the handle behind his back and soon found a comfortable walking rhythm. Ahead, at the base of the distant blue-green bluffs, he spotted a plume of dust moving closer and closer. The plume soon turned into a black spot, and then the spot changed into an animal with four legs, a horse. The horse was galloping and kicking up dust behind it, and it grew and grew as it approached, and Ben could see a man on top of the horse wearing a black cowboy hat and a long black duster flapping in the breeze.

The horseman pulled up next to him. The horse stomped, its mouth frothy. On the man's chest hung a silver star.

'You the law around here?' Ben asked.

The man looked down at Ben from under his broad black hat. His eyes were pale and flat, and his gaze aimed not-quite-right.

'I am,' he said, blinking, which was when Ben realized the lawman was blind.

'What you got there?'

'Nothing,' Ben said.

Sara Koepke had tiptoed off a ways and now stood still as a statue on the edge of the forest. She smiled brightly, her eyebrows up. The lawman leaned across his saddle horn and the leather squeaked. He let his flat gaze fall to Ben, or almost to Ben. Just to the right of Ben.

'I got reports of a man turning to a fish that I happen to be investigating the death of,' he said.

Ben felt all the blood leave his face. He took a deep breath and balanced himself properly over his two feet to keep from falling down. Sara waved from behind the sumac bush, still smiling wildly.

'Is it the death of the *man-turning-to-a-fish*?' she shouted from the bushes. 'Or the death of the *reports* of a man-turning-to-a-fish that you're investigating?'

The lawman tilted his head like a confused dog. 'Who's that?'

'Who's what?'

'You didn't hear?'

'I heard you,' Ben said. 'I heard me.'

'A wood nymph,' Sara shouted from behind the bushes.

'Yes!' the lawman said, and smiled.

'Yes, what?' Ben said.

'Was the man a man when he died?' Sara asked. 'Or was he a man-turned-fish when he died? And did he die at all, or is it merely a dead report that you're investigating?'

The lawman screwed up his face under the big black brim of his hat. 'You're confusing me,' he said, 'whoever you are.'

'It's not me, whoever or whatever you're talking to,' Ben said.

'Let me smell them hands,' the lawman said.

'These?' Ben held them up for inspection.

The lawman took each of Ben's hands in his and lifted it to his face, sniffed, carefully turned it over, and sniffed again.

'Mmm,' he said when he let the second hand go. The saddle leather squeaked, and again he squinted just to the right of Ben.

'Well?' Sara said from the bushes.

'Well, I don't smell nothin',' he said.

'You don't?' Ben smelled his own hands and they smelled very fishy.

Sara shouted, 'But that don't mean he's innocent!' and laughed.

'But that don't mean you're innocent,' the sheriff repeated.

'I didn't kill anybody!' Ben said. 'Not a fish or man or a report!'

The blind lawman shrugged. 'Maybe. Maybe not. But you best hope I never run into you again, because I just might hang you from the highest tree.' He liked the sound of this so he said it again as he turned his horse and began to ride away. 'From the highest tree!'

Ben watched him ride away until he grew small, then tiny, and finally disappeared. Sara Koepke had come back from behind the bush and stood next to him.

'You trying to get me in trouble?' he asked, but he couldn't be angry because she looked so flushed with laughter and also she kissed him on the sun-warmed top of his head when he bent down to pick up the handle of the wagon.

ODDLY ENOUGH, THINGS HAD BEGUN to make a little bit of sense to Ben. He'd fallen in love with Sara Koepke when he was very young, and, beginning when he was nineteen and lasting for six years, he'd carried on with her like a madman right under his brother's nose. In the last year, Ben had abandoned the main house for a cot in the old chicken house at the edge of the yard. He would work with Danny during the day and in the evening eat a dinner Sara cooked—then he'd spend the rest of the night drowning in his solitude whether she managed a visit or not. In despair, he finally broke free and fled, and once he got started he didn't stop. He ran a long way—a long way from home and from himself—and spent his entire adult life hiding from desire and regret. Did he really think he could get home again so easily? On a jet plane and in a rental car?

After so long, was there any other way home besides the strange way?

He began to walk along the road. Sara Koepke walked ahead of him, and she wore high-heeled shoes and tight short shorts and a halter top. He admired her shoulders and calves, and the shape of her bottom, and the nice way she'd done her hair. He blinked against the sweat and glare. He looked to his feet, walking on a dusty road now, the macadam gone, then up again and the country had changed and was no longer curved and dressed in summer green, but bare and stark and flat, and the familiar rail fence had disappeared, too.

'Where are we?' Ben asked.

Sara pointed to a wooden grave marker next to the trail.

> *An Indian Squaw*
> *June 27, Killed by a fall*
> *From a horse*
> *Near this place*

Calm be her sleep

Sweet be her rest

Be kind to the Indian

The grave looked recently dug. Sara knelt next to it. Her rear end twitched back and forth as her hands sifted through the loose dirt.

'What are you doing?' Ben asked.

'You wouldn't believe the things people bury in graves,' she said.

'Dead bodies?'

She shrugged. 'And sometimes other cool stuff.'

Her quick little hands had uncovered a tin box big enough for a baby, maybe. She lifted it out of the grave and pried open the lid. 'See?' she said, opening it. Inside was no decomposed child but vials of medicine and a note.

'*Dear Doctor,*' she read. '*I took almost but not quite half. We lost a boy last week and my girl is suffering with the shakes. I'm afraid my wife is next. I promise not to tell anyone else about this here medicine.*'

Sara took a couple of vials and shoved them into her pocket, and replaced the rest, with the note, and re-lidded the tin box, and laid it back in the grave. She pulled loose gray soil over the top, and packed it down with a rock.

They walked on, following a trail along a dry creek bottom. The road made a bend and climbed up a hill, and along the trail lay carcasses of mules and oxen and horses in various stages of decomposition, and farther up an old man with a tattered coverlet wrapped over his shoulders rode by on a jaded horse. He looked pale and haggard and a corner of the coverlet trailed in the dust.

'Flux and scurvy ahead,' he said as he passed.

Farther up, they could hear shouting, and see a trail of dust leading to a line of wagons. Men shouted at oxen, lashing them, and women and children walked behind or to the side in clouds of blinding dust. Sometimes the boys led broken animals up the hill or the women chocked wagon wheels to give the oxen a blow. A man with a baby in his arms, in the midst of thick dust, urged his oxen up up up! One wagon uncoupled, rolled backward, women and children in it, screaming. There was a great clamor. Luckily the wagon hit a dead mule, stopped, and everybody laughed.

Over the top of the hill, past the line of wagons, Ben and Sara and Danny the Tuna passed more grave markers, all of them fresh. Sara had to get down on her hands and knees and check each and every one for booty, but all had bodies.

'You're going to get sick doing that,' Ben said.

'Wait 'til you're hungry on the way to the sea,' she said, 'and I find beans. Who'll be sick then?'

They walked all night long. His feet hurt and in his sleeplessness he began to grow confused again. He'd come home to forgive himself and to begin to be able to love his brother again, so why was he going to the sea? To let a dead fish go free? Part of him hoped he'd suddenly wake up back home in our nation's capital to the sounds of his auto-start coffee maker, the smell of fresh brew, a day as a professional technocrat lying neatly ahead, but he was pretty sure by now that he'd come too far to ever wake up again into a such a clear amnesiac bliss. The heart was an easy place to get lost and he suspected it was only going to get worse. He resolved to keep going for as long as he had the strength, and then even a little bit longer. They passed through hill country on a winding road, and sometime before the moon rose that night they heard a mule slip over the edge and fall to the river below. The trail led them out of the hills onto a vast silver plain. The procession of emigrants thinned and spread out, and soon the moon set again and they were walking blindly in the dark, and Ben's feet began to hurt a lot, and he closed his eyes and opened them and couldn't see any difference, the night had grown so dark. He could hear Sara panting behind him, and sometimes next to him, and he fell asleep for moments as he walked, and once when he opened his eyes he saw a straight horizontal line in front of him, thin as wire. It gleamed brightly and Ben lifted his hand to keep from walking into it.

'What?' Sara said, bumping into him from behind and almost tripping on the wagon.

'Nothing,' he said, and started to walk again. But the wire grew still sharper, clearer, and brighter. Soon it was glowing like phosphorus, a neck-high clothesline stretched across his dark path. Frustrated, he continued to wave his free arm in front of him as he walked.

'What are you doing?' Sara asked.

'Can't you see that?'

'What?'

Ben stopped walking. 'That!' he said.

Sara stepped up next to him and looked into the darkness. 'I don't see it,' she said.

Ben squinted at the line, and blinked, and looked again. It had begun to widen and shimmer, and then it changed into something else entirely. Below the perfectly straight horizontal line the land lay flat and dark. Above it, the sky pinked with dawn.

'Oh, christ,' Ben said.

'What?'

He'd been swinging at the horizon.

'Nothing,' he said.

They slept and woke that afternoon on a vast grassland plain. Ben felt as if his dry tongue didn't fit in his mouth anymore, and his stomach had shrunk to a hard little nut. Danny the Tuna lay covered with flies in the wagon. Ben looked around. During the night they must have walked off the two-track trail and now he wanted to find it. He didn't know why. He didn't know where it went and all he'd seen on it was human misery. Nevertheless, he ran frantically this way and that, looking. He ran up to the top of a rise, then back down again. What was it about the trail that drew him? Perhaps it was the knowledge that it had ends, and that each end touched *someplace!* Here, in the middle of the grassy sea, with no trail, only land extending forever to more land, to more grassy sea, his certainty failed him. He felt panicked and overwhelmed—

and the resolve he'd felt yesterday to keep plodding along had evaporated. He could see a jet plane high in the sky and he imagined the passengers peering out their windows watching him run pathetically back and forth like a frightened mouse. He fell to his knees and caught his breath. He fought back tears and in a sudden burst of self-pity he screamed at the sky in a voice that seemed someone else's. Hadn't he decided to do the right thing, goddamit, and come home, goddamit, after so many years? Hadn't he been just a little proud, goddamit, sitting on the jet plane soaring through the sky above the continent, sipping gin, proud of how brave, goddamit, he was to go home after so many years? Hadn't he felt good and innocent and successful, goddamit? His life redeemed by the good decision to leave home years ago, and now redeemed by his brave decision to come home again? And whatever other way you wanted to look at it, hadn't he lived a virtuous life in our nation's capital, staying away from other men's wives and trying not to offend racial or ethnic minorities?

If so, then how could he be where he was now? Lost on the vast trackless heart of a big-hearted country?

'*Nigger nigger nigger!*' he screamed into the impassive blue sky, at the puffy little cartoon clouds. '*Chink chink chink!*'

Something answered. He listened. What? Was the hawk laughing at him? Or Coyote? No, Sara Koepke was. He could hear her. And what a joyful laugh! His panic turned gradually to embarrassment. Because there she was, sitting by the wagon down in the coulee on the old road leading toward the pale blue hills and the river. And there was the old familiar rail fence.

'I'm sorry,' he said, ashamed. 'I thought we were lost.'

'I guess you did,' she said. She'd taken off her high heels and now stood in her bare feet, her red toenails dulled behind dust.

'Wait here,' she said, 'while I go pee.'

She disappeared off the road and into the brush. Ben stared at the fence. Now he knew why it was familiar. It was the same one he and Danny built years ago. He remembered pulling the old rotting rail fence out and digging new post holes. He remembered sawing and nailing up the rails. He remembered working shirtless, skin smelling of summer sunshine, taking turns with the posthole digger, with the big iron tamping bar, feeling his muscles grow as he worked, his bones stretching toward manhood. They dug and tamped to the rhythm of radio songs, gyrating and hooting and making the big exaggerated gestures of young men. They made odd noises with their mouths and body parts, they laughed with glee. They talked in their own shorthand, with their own intonations and sounds that conjured people and stories they knew.

Ben turned to see where the fence bumped into an old chicken house—marvelous wonder!—he could see two skinny young men wearing shorts and boots, bent over their tools, weak with laughter. He crept closer and recognized Danny, standing straight now, saw him flick his straw-hair back, lift the posthole digger and slam it back into the hole. He pulled apart the handles, squeezed them together again. He lifted it and emptied the black soil onto a pile. Then he slid the digger back down the hole. His movements showed natural grace, and while he worked the digger around in the hole, young Ben himself lifted the new treated post, held it poised above the hole, his lean body flexing, the muscles visible under his skin, and just as Danny pulled the last bit of soil from the hole, Ben dropped in the new post. He stood next to it, measured the height, heart-high. Yessir.

Standing, watching, Ben was reminded of how he and his brother had worked together like two hands of the same body, in perfect coordination, knowing what the other was going to do by some invisible connection of the flesh. Not only in simple jobs like digging a post hole and placing the post, but also in the big jobs. A slight gesture, a step, a facial expression carried with it the priorities for the day, the big plan.

Then the two working boys vanished and Ben stood in the road alone waiting for Sara Koepke. The sun seemed too bright suddenly, and his forehead beaded with sweat. Could it be his brother was really dead?

He looked at the wagon. The tuna seemed to have grown, its sides overlapping the lip of the Radio Flyer. He waved the flies away from Danny's face, Danny's gold eyes.

'Look,' he said, 'the fence we built.'

But Danny didn't blink. He lay there, fish-dead. Christ. How depressing. A puff of cloud made a shadow that moved swiftly across the valley. Cows bawled somewhere. Calves blatted. Sara was still in the bushes peeing and an old man approached, thin to emaciation, narrow shoulders, curved nose, large ears set far back, lantern jawed, a face in repose, passively inhuman, bloodless, petrified . . . Yet Ben could see he looked vaguely familiar.

'You either believe in general history,' the man said, '*New people came, and things changed.* Or—'

'Grandpa?'

'Boy?'

They embraced but the old man was so thin and frail as to hardly exist. Ben let him go, gently, and he began to walk. Ben fell in beside him, matching him stride for stride.

'Or you believe in a more personal history:' his grandpa continued, '*My father disappeared into the wilderness with nothing . . . and he walked out a wealthy man!*'

They passed through an old mining town. Dark and abandoned buildings stood next to holes like bites in the earth. They passed bleached skeletons chained to a tree, iron collars still locked around their fleshless necks.

'What are these?'

'Slaves.'

'Isn't slavery over?'

The old man nodded. 'For them boys, I s'pose so.'

They rounded a bend and descended a hill to a quaint-looking barn and farmhouse lit by moonlight at the edge of the forest.

'It's the home farm,' Ben said. 'Everywhere I go, I come back to it.'

'Look closer.'

Ben did. The white picket fence around the yard sprouted bizarre ornaments. As they approached, the moonlight grew brighter and the ornaments revealed themselves to be human heads.

'My god!' Ben said.

His grandfather was quiet. Music drifted out from an open window of the farmhouse. Bach on the piano, a celebration of God, of heaven, of the best and most beautiful the human mind could conjure. A child's sweet voice sang along.

'That's me,' the old man said. 'My teacher's playing the piano. She used to say that when I played the piano I had to decide to love God or to hate Him—anything in between meant I hadn't got out of bed yet.'

They stood at the gate and Ben listened to the music as he examined the heads on each fence post, moving from one post to the next to look at the desiccated faces and long black Indian hair.

'My old man—your great-grandfather Clarence—had another theory on religion,' Grandpa said. *'Cut off fifteen Injun heads and a thousand and fifty will either disappear on their own account or line up ready and willing to do the work of the Lord.'*

Ben felt sick to his stomach. He turned away from the house and the heads and looked toward the river, at the spring fields cultivated for corn and oats. The young alfalfa shivered in the breeze. Grandpa spit, and kicked at the soil at his feet. 'Look,' he said, and he bent down to unearth a bone. Lifted it and gave it to

Ben, who passed it back and forth from hand to hand, feeling its weight.

'What is it?'

'Shinbone, I s'pose.'

'It's little.'

'Injun child.'

'How do you know?'

'Pops went Injun huntin',' he said. 'Cut off their feet. I don't recall why they did that. Money, I s'pose. Somebody was buying.'

Ben rubbed his thumb over the sawed end of the bone, clean and square. He was horrified. 'Children?'

'Pops said they were the children of killers. Alive, they'd torment us forever.'

'That's terrible,' Ben said.

Grandpa shrugged. 'Injuns ain't hardly something you worry about anymore, is they?'

'No, but—'

'Good.' Grandpa said. 'Then maybe it done some good to kill 'em. All I know is I didn't sleep well most of my life. Bad dreams. I married a half-Injun woman who forgave me my blood and loved me madly but sometimes even she couldn't stand me once the sun went down. Only fishing seemed to calm my nerves.'

'I had no idea,' Ben said. But when he looked up from the ground he saw a rainbow on the distant horizon. The corn had sprouted and now stood waist-high in dark green rows stretching all the way to the river. Blue-green oats carried wind in waves across the breast of the hill, and the alfalfa lay in curving windrows to dry in the sun.

'Hey.' It was Sara Koepke, back from the bushes. 'What are you staring at?'

Ben shook his head. 'There used to be skulls on the fence here,' he said. 'On this fence before Danny and I built a new one.'

'Things happen,' she said.

'What?'

'Don't ruin this for me, okay?' Her voice was compelling.

'Ruin what? Ghosts everywhere, and a dead brother-turned-fish on a wagon?'

Sara Koepke puffed her lips in a pout. 'What did you come home for, anyway?'

'I love Danny,' Ben said. 'And I didn't want to lose him until I had to.'

'You read that somewhere?' She stooped to pick up the handle of the wagon. She began to walk.

'Where are you going?' he called after her.

'To the sea,' she said, 'Wasn't that the plan?'

'Yes, but—'

'With a quick stop at the river,' she said. The wagon axle squeaked and dust rose behind the black plastic wheels.

Ben didn't follow immediately. He stood still as a statue, feeling his weight on his heels. He tried to remember the gladness he felt seeing his brother, his living brother, standing in the bright hallway of the farmhouse, but the dead fish smell gave him a touch of nausea. He tried to find the strength he'd need to see his brother again. He took a deep breath through his mouth, then another, felt his chest expand and contract with new resolve.

It's about *doing*, his grandma had said. It's about *loving*.

As though she'd read his mind, Sara glanced back over her shoulder and flashed him one of her outrageously flirtatious smiles. 'At the river I'll give you one last shot at showing a girl a good time,' she said, and winked.

BEN WOKE IN THE MORNING with the sun streaming through the bedroom window. His grandma's flowered wallpaper had been removed, as had the white paint on the woodwork, where now a lovely wood grain shone under varnish. Beautifully refinished maple floors, too. And outside the window the grass had grown crazy long, the birds and bugs chattered their summer sounds. Cows bawled in the hollow. Ben felt the prickly opening of his pores and the sweat began even before he dared peek out into the hallway.

Only a black cat that should have been dead years ago lay in the patch of sunlight on the orange carpet at the top of the stairs. Ben stepped quickly over it and headed downstairs. In the living room, he saw none of his grandma's old yellow magazine pictures that she liked to tape to the walls. Pictures of cute little girls, of snowy mountains, of flowers. None of her piles of other people's laundry, either. What a relief! And then—even better—a note on the kitchen table in his brother's hand: *We thought we'd let you sleep. Hope you feel better this morning. We're at the river. Come on down!*

Ben drank some water—actually, he drank glass after glass of water. It was odd they hadn't woken him—he wondered what they said to each other. He didn't feel sick but he did feel nervous. Also a little light-headed so he knew he should eat something. He found an apple in the fridge and washed it and then headed out the front door to his rental car. But something told him that if he got into the car to drive, he wouldn't stop at the river. He'd just keep going. He'd drive back to the airport and catch an early flight.

He bit into the cold apple and walked bravely past the car and the barn and down the gravel driveway to the county highway leading north to the river beach. The humidity soaked his shirt and paled the sky, turned the distant hills blue-gray and fuzzy. He tried in vain to imagine winter. Hadn't it been winter just last night? The memory nagged but the familiar walk reassured him. He dropped off the highway just before the bridge and took the road through the slough, which smelled of black water and wet wood. The exercise made him feel good. Whatever he'd done that caused suffering could be forgiven with a brisk walk and a swim. He knew that was an absurd notion but he listened to the blackbirds screeching and felt the jungle air of a tropical continent and couldn't help his optimism. He imagined seeing Danny again today. He'd walk right up to him. He'd embrace him. He'd shake his hand. They'd laugh and squint into the sunshine. They'd swim together into the current and the future would begin. Why not? They were two brothers on earth who loved each other.

The road came out of the swamp at a sand bar stretching for almost a mile along the inside of the river's westward curve. The tea-brown water lay smooth and wide, reflecting the bluff on the far side, the crowns of oak and hickory and grapevines and sumac, and the sandstone cliff pocked with swallows' nests. Under the smooth surface of the river, the current moved fast. And beneath that, the sandy bottom was always changing. A place knee-deep one day might be thirty feet the next. A place ankle-deep now may suddenly collapse into a churning, bottomless hole.

Still, the beach was lovely, and he could see two human figures at the far end of the long strip of yellow sand. Puffy clouds hung in the sultry air like friendly ghosts. Ben took his shoes off and felt the warm sand on the bottom of his feet. He walked toward the figures and as he got closer he could see Sara Koepke lying on a towel. A hundred yards beyond her, Danny stood fishing on the downstream edge of the sandbar, his back to Ben.

Ben walked quietly up to Sara. She had her eyes closed, and he stood looking down at her face, smooth skin around her eyes and mouth. He closed his eyes and tried to maintain his balance. The sweat on his temples felt hot and then suddenly cold. When he opened his eyes again, Sara was still twenty-five years younger than she'd been yesterday. He couldn't even wonder at how it had happened, because he felt everything coming back, filling his veins, all the desire he'd been so unable to control. He looked down the beach to his brother, who cast a lure out into the water, and who hadn't noticed Ben yet. Ben knelt down at Sara's feet, took a handful of dry sand and let it pour through his fist onto her foot. She opened her eyes, made a pleasurable noise, and then closed them again. He crawled up along her leg, past her waist, and glancing again at his brother, leaned down over her face and kissed her lips lightly. Then he kissed her neck, keeping one eye on his brother, blurry now in the liquid heat rising off the sand. After each kiss he thought *now I will stop, now I will stop*, but he couldn't. He kissed each nipple through her nylon suit.

'Please,' she said. He could see tears forming in the corner of her eyes. He sat up. His brother was still fishing.

'I can't leave him,' she said.

Ben touched her thigh, very lightly, just the tips of his fingers.

'I'm pregnant,' she said.

Ben swallowed, breathed, aware of the gulls gliding in arcs across the sky, aware of the breeze on his back and his tongue gone fat and dry so he couldn't speak, couldn't ask the question. She answered anyway.

'It's Danny's.'

The tears fattened in the corners of her eyes but still had not begun to roll down her cheeks.

'Jesuschrist,' she said, 'aren't you going to say anything?'

Ben shook his head, fighting back the big wall of fire rising from his belly. He turned to see his brother still fishing, still unaware.

'He's ecstatic,' Sara said. 'That's the good part. He can hardly wait to tell you.'

Ben tried to stand, but felt suddenly cold. He shivered and his brain seemed to twist like the crown of a tree in a storm. He felt himself teetering, and then falling. The puffy clouds spun and the river tipped vertical and when he landed the hot sand burned his cheek.

SO THIS WAS IT—this was the strange trip home. He'd been right about some things. Like how there was no turning back once he got started. But really all he'd done so far is come home. All he'd done is greet Sara in the afternoon, sleep a fever-charged dream in which he'd seen spirits and walked into memories. All he'd done is get out of bed and take a feverish sleepwalk in his boxers, to bump into his brother in the hallway. His brother! All he'd done is talk with Danny for the first time in twenty-five years. About ghosts and how weird it all was. Then he sat down in the kitchen late and drank whiskey alone. All he'd done is go back to sleep, then wake to walk to the river, where he saw Sara, where he shivered and burned, and then collapsed into a feverish memory.

Hadn't he stayed away so long because he knew, *he knew* that if he came home again he'd feel the heat, the sand, the kiss? Feel the chill all over again? Feel his betrayal hollow out his insides and fill him with a big empty wind?

Perhaps. But he hadn't been quite right about that. Because the wind was far from empty after it had sifted through the crowns of the oak and hickory forest, across the blue-green oats and purple alfalfa, over the dewy grass between the bluffs to the fat blue river and yellow sand bar. It carried the smells of his life, the elements that made him, and coming home was breathing them all in until he was so full he could burst. *A boy dove for a girl and caught her slippery ankle in his hand and pulled her toward him under the water. He lifted her in both arms and gathered his strength and carried her up out of the river, up the sandy beach, where he lay her down gently on a towel.* Aaah, she said, my Tarzan! and sighed, and he began to kiss her neck and shoulder and side, around her breasts to her belly, and then across to her hip, a hundred kisses down her hip to the outside of her thigh, and ten kisses more to her knee and over to the inside of her thigh, where he kissed and touched with the tip of his nose her downy skin up, up, up toward the magic edges of her swimsuit.

He laid his cheek on the mound of her sex, and he breathed deeply all of her.

'Jesus.'

'What?'

'Too much!' he said, and ran panicked back to the water. She called his name. He dove in and swam and swam and swam into the current, then back with it, and he didn't come up until his lungs were burning, and when he did, he could see her halfway across the sandbar, no longer by herself, but with Danny, sure, and she was small and flat-chested, and she and Danny were running away from him, and Grandpa stood fishing out on the point of the bar, the band of his brown fedora stained with sweat, his khakis rolled up to his knees, his red flannel long-sleeve shirt buttoned up to the collar.

The sky was blue and the clouds puffy and the river felt good, his skin wet, and he watched Danny and Sara Koepke run away, laughing, and calling back to him, and laughing again. He ran out of the water and chased them over the hot sand, screaming *'Wait! Wait!'* until he was sure blood vessels were popping in his brain. He chased them to the end of the sand and into the stinky slough, feet sinking in the slimy mud until he had to swim. The tangle of branches over the water made shade and the moss grew thick on the trunks and the water turned black as night. Ahead he heard shouting and giggling, and he screamed *'Wait!'* again, and he heard his name whispered and kept swimming, chasing, and soon his limbs tired and he gasped, shouting *'Wait!'* with the black water spilling over his chin into his mouth. He swallowed some. He tried to grab a branch to keep from going under but got another mouthful. He remembered his grandma saying that slough water is the bath water of ghosts and to stay out of it. But here he was in it, almost under it, and he felt a tangle of submerged branches with his feet, and he thought about catfish the size of men, and his own mother and father dead down under somewhere beneath his feet, and he heard Danny and Sara Koepke laughing and then saw them playing in the branches of a tree. He screamed and screamed and swallowed more water. Why don't they wait for him? Why do they always run away from him? Sara in her blue two-piece and chestnut hair, Danny lanky and white and strong, hair the color of straw, with their mother's full lips, thank the Lord, as his grandma always said, a real mouth, not some hatchet slash.

Ben swallowed more black water and thought of crocodiles even though Grandpa said that was hogwash, and so he thought of actual hogwash, swimming in hogwash, and he could smell it, pig shit, and taste it, and he could see Danny and Sara Koepke climbing in the trees above the water, hand-over-hand like monkeys over the water, moving through the branches of the trees that formed a lovely web over the water, which tasted like ghost pee in his mouth, and he kicked wildly to keep his head above the water (even though he was afraid to kick his mother or father down under there somewhere.) Danny swung down, and Sara, above him, eyes big as platters, disappeared suddenly as the world turned black. He went under with the lovely vision of her face, her eyes, and then he felt Danny's hand on his arm above the elbow, and a jerk upward, and more water in his mouth. Danny pulled him out of the water and draped him over a low branch, lifted him while he coughed and coughed and gagged and coughed, hanging him over the branch like a limp sheet, the branch across his waist, under him, holding him a few feet above the black ghost-piss water.

'Idiot,' Danny said. 'I said don't follow us.'

'You called me!'

'Well, we didn't mean it,' Sara said.

Then they helped him back to the beach, where he stood with his grandpa, then sat at his grandpa's feet and played with five dead fish, different stages of wet and dry, of shiny and dull, in the sand. He lined them up from big to small, turned them over, then over again, covering them with sand, as his grandma sometimes covered them with bread crumbs before frying them.

'I'm cooking them, Grandpa. See how I'm cooking them?'

Grandpa looked down at him, amused. He dropped a knife and said, 'Why don't you clean them rather than play with them, Benji.'

So Ben used the knife to scrape off the scales, doing how Grandpa had taught him. Scraping both sides and the back, and the yellow bellies, then slicing each from vent to gills and fingering out the guts, then rubbing his thumbnail back and forth along the fold to remove all the grape jelly that lined the spine. He watched the pieces of intestine and heart and liver and pink cluster of eggs, and chunks of grape float away in the smooth flat river that reflected sandstone bluffs from the far shore. He washed the fish in the river and set them in the bucket so they wouldn't cover again with sand, and he washed his hands in the river but couldn't get the fish smell off. The summer after he fled the farm for good he'd cleaned halibut in heavy seas that sent him sliding on his knees from beam to beam, knife in his hand, sleepless, using numb fingers to reach past the bowels of each fish and scoop out two clean triangular gonads. On and on through the night, they'd work, stacking the fish like cordwood in the ice below deck, resetting and hauling long lines, gaffing fish as big as men until the deck was shin deep with new catch. Sometimes the whiff of a half-decayed cod on the long line made him bend over the rail to puke, barely pausing in his work to do so. Twenty-four, thirty-six, forty-eight hours without sleep—but he learned he could bear up if he had to. He was a man now, able to endure terrible discomfort because, well, because that's what the job required that he do. Skipper called him a *fish-cleaning motherfucker, all right*, and one summer day many years before when he was a teenager he stood at a retaining wall with his back to the water, cleaning an undersized, illegal musky. A quick thunderstorm grew over the top of the pines and sent an arm of lightning into the lake behind him. At the same time, a couple of electric fingers shot out of the lake into the back of both his thighs. *Yikes!* He leaped toward the heavens . . . but came safely down to earth again, not dead. Barely even burned.

Danny had seen the whole thing, and laughed and laughed and laughed.

A little lightning and you scream like a baby! he'd teased. *What would you do if something really shocking happened?*

'Hey!' Sara Koepke called. She stood fishing on the downstream point of the sandbar, standing where Grandpa had been standing. She stood naked, though, her middle-aged body freckled and surprisingly taut, her shoulder-length hair wet. Had they already made love? Ben didn't remember. She moved as though they had, relaxed, unselfconscious, without coyness. She waded ankle deep in the river to be able to cast farther out.

Ben relaxed into the shallow water, tipped his head back and closed his eyes to the merciless sky. When he opened them again, Sara had moved out farther, thigh-deep now. Her hair still chestnut but streaked with gray, her breasts like upside-down bells. She cast gracefully out into the smooth water.

'Where's Danny?' he yelled.

She turned and scanned the water to find him Ben. 'Look,' she shouted. 'Stop messing with me, okay? Why can't we just have fun?'

The hurt in her eyes made him feel cruel. He sat in shallow water, his back to the current, holding himself firm by digging his heels into the sand. He didn't know what to say. The river stretched between them like a dream, blue and smooth and broad, flat between round bluffs.

'Can you hear me?' she shouted.

His head was the only thing visible above the water and he nodded.

'God forgive me!' she shouted. 'But this is a dream I've had for a long time.'

'What?'

'That he's dead!' Her voice carried over the river and echoed off the bluffs and came back again. 'And that you're back here at the river with me!'

Ben felt stupid, as though he should have understood. He wanted to apologize but didn't.

'I loved him!' she yelled. 'But I always loved you, too!'

Ben felt the blood rush to his face. He could have said the exact same words.

'If I killed him,' he said, and then stopped. He listened to the echo, the unreal sound of both his words and his voice. He started again: 'If I killed him . . .'

She looked at him across the water and even from this distance her eyes magnified the sky and the river, beckoning him with the same power they'd always had over him. 'For godsake, Ben,' she said, 'Think of something else. Think anything you have to think! Just please don't ruin our chance to finally be happy.'

AND HE MIGHT HAVE, would have, could have, of course—were it not that he had bad dreams. For while they slept that night on the edge of the slough on a little bed of twigs, tucked around one another for warmth while Danny the Tuna lay cold in the wagon, Ben dreamed again that he woke in the farmhouse, in his childhood bed, and this time he heard a lamp crash downstairs and the glass break. He heard the legs of the dining room table skid across the floor. The house shook with stomping. Then the sound of wood splintering, cracking.

He leapt out of bed and ran out of his room and started down the stairs. He turned the corner on the bottom landing and stopped just before running into Sara Koepke.

'Would you look at that!' she said.

Ben did. Over her shoulder he could see three cows had crowded into the living room through the front door. Ben pushed past Sara and waved his arms. The cows ran out of the living room and into the kitchen toward the open back door but the three of them tried to get out at once. They got stuck, and the house shook, and while Sara shrieked, Ben pulled himself over the cow jam, climbed the knotted backs to get in front of them. He hung by his fingers from the woodwork over the door and kicked the cows' curly faces until two of them backed up and one could pass through the doorway into the backyard, then another and another until the house was again free of cows.

'Oh my god,' Sara said, hands on her hips, surveying the damage. 'This is all I need.'

The furniture had been tipped over and broken. The wood floor was wet with urine and spotted with manure. Except for the sound of Ben's breathing, the house was silent.

That afternoon, they scrubbed the cow shit off the wall and floor, repaired the furniture they could repair, and made a pile outside of the irreparable. Or Ben did. Sara Koepke sat on the kitchen table in a black leotard and assumed a sequence of yoga positions.

'Won't Ivy and Jessie want to come home for the funeral?' he asked her.

'No,' Sara said. 'They're quite busy and if they come home don't you think they are going to ask questions?'

Ben was rinsing a bucket in the kitchen sink, rinsing a rag in clean water. He turned and looked into her eyes, which were light green and bottomless, also upside down.

'Are you insane?' he said.

She ignored the question. 'Remember all the bones in the pasture?'

'No,' he said.

'On our walk? And even more up in a cave I know. You should remember that cave, too, come to think of it.'

'I should?'

She changed positions. Ben looked at her rubber limbs, her curved spine connecting her round bottom to her breasts and shoulders.

'We called it the bone cave. Your brother's pun. You lost your virginity there.'

Ben remembered but didn't want to. 'Oh,' he said.

She slid off the table and took a step toward Ben.

'And our last time? When we met there? You were so upset, you . . . And then you left.'

Ben turned back to the window again. Dusk, and he could feel her behind him. He could hear her fussing with her leotard— taking it off? He was afraid to turn and look, kept his eyes aimed out the window at the valley softened with dusk. He felt her hands on his shoulders. They smelled like fish but he was terribly aroused anyway, even trembling. She slid her hands down over his shoulders, down his arms, to his hands.

'I wish I could believe in God,' she said,

It wasn't what he expected her to say.

'What would you pray for?'

'Me,' she said, and sighed. 'I'm a widow now. What will I do?' She pulled one of Ben's hands behind his back and put it on the mound between her legs. He quickly pulled his hand back.

'It burns!' he said.

'Yes. Terribly.'

Darkness fell, and the far hillside twinkled with the thousand yellow campfires of the Union army, and row upon row of ghostly tents lit by lanterns.

'Oh shit,' she said.

'I better go outside and say goodnight to the soldiers,' he said, and without looking at her he turned and crossed the room to the door. Outside, the campfires had blinked out, the tents disappeared, and Ben was left standing in the middle of a dark yard. He thought he heard Danny's laughter.

'Danny?'

No answer.

'Danny, I'm home!'

Again he heard his brother from somewhere in the bushes.

'Danny?'

The laughter stopped. So did the sound of the crickets and peepers.

'Danny, where are you?'

Come find me! Danny said, no longer in the bushes.

Ben looked but he couldn't see. 'Where?'

Over here! The voice came from behind the pile of broken living room and kitchen furniture.

Ben ran over and began to toss pieces of chair and couch and table here and there but to no avail. He couldn't find his brother. Finally, he stood tired and out of breath. He called again for his brother but only an owl answered from the dead elm tree behind him. He threw himself onto the dewy grass in despair. He'd gone so far, and now he'd come back. Yet where was he? And where was Danny? He felt cold in the damp grass and shivered, and then he felt hot and sat up and stared at the unending heavens. Was there nothing else but this? Crazy hot? Crazy cold? Night after night after night? The same goddam moon and the same goddam stars?

The heavens don't show me shit, he thought, and so he yelled: 'Show me something!'

The star-freckled face of heaven stared down at him mutely.

Ben shook his fist. 'Show me something I haven't seen before!'

As if in answer to his challenge, the stars twinkled out and the long summer night passed into an autumn morning, and Ben found himself walking in the woods with a rifle, hunting deer. The dry oak leaves made a thick, brown carpet and the noise of his every step reverberated through the forest.

Well, Ben thought, I suppose this is something.

He walked for a long time and just when he'd given up on seeing a buck, he passed a little green plant sticking up through the leaves, and the plant said, *Eat me!*

Ben stopped. He was a teenager again, and he knew this Coyote story but he couldn't remember exactly what happened. He was awfully hungry, though, after a long day hunting in the woods.

Eat me! the plant said again.

Ben reached down, pinched the tender green stem with his fingers, lifted the plant to his mouth, and took a small bite. Mmmm. Not bad. He ate all of it.

Almost immediately he began to break wind. Long cool silent leaks. Short blasts. Roaring goose calls. He did so many that soon he felt himself lose weight, as if all the solid inside him had turned to gas, and the gas was escaping fast. Then he actually began to float. At first just a few inches above the leaves on the forest floor. It was fun! He tooted still more and rose still higher. A foot, two feet, then higher! He grabbed a bush to keep from floating away, but the brittle twigs broke off in his hands and he began to grow frightened. He drifted into the branches of oak trees and there he needed to hang on with all of his strength to keep from floating even higher.

Then, just as suddenly as the farts began, they ended. Slowly he felt his body solidify again, gain weight, and he lowered gently out of the forest canopy onto the ground below, where he sat, shaken but unhurt. He was still hungry, though, and cold and he heard a distant honking. Through the naked tree branches he saw actual geese flying in a V across the gray sky.

Then he heard another little voice say, *Eat me!*

A pretty green plant sprouted among the yellow birch leaves.

Eat me!

'No thanks, little plant,' Ben said, getting to his feet. But he picked the plant anyway and put it in his pocket. He didn't know what time it was, afternoon or morning, or even what day, but he felt a terrible urgency to get home. He dropped down the ridge and came out of the woods near where the herd of red cattle stood in clover. Danny stood under an apple tree chewing on a piece of grass. He wore baggy shorts and an open blue denim jacket over a red flowered Hawaiian shirt. He squatted to watch the cattle graze under the brim of a wool plaid haystacker hat. He was looking for bad hooves, for pinkeye, for the shadow of ribs in an old cow.

Unnoticed, Ben snuck up behind his brother. He debated with himself whether to talk to him or not. He wanted to ask him more questions and hear again his voice. He wanted to stand next to him in the field. But he was still mad at Danny for hiding from him so he dropped the magic plant and watched as his brother heard the plea, *Eat me!* He watched Danny pick up the plant, eat it, and begin passing gas. He watched Danny gasp, lift up off the ground, reach in vain for the branches of the apple tree, and keep rising. He watched a gust take Danny even higher, and he watched as Danny faded to a small black dot high above the valley floor that drifted south on a high wind. Soon he was out of sight and dusk was falling.

Frightened and wracked by sudden guilt, Ben fled down the valley toward the house in the dark. It seemed to take him all night, for by the time he arrived, the windows were lit yellow against a dawn sky. He could see Sara Koepke's pretty head in the window above the kitchen sink, and as he approached he thought she saw him too, and waved, and Ben's knees grew weak in anticipation of passion. It took almost all of his strength—and who knew how long—to walk around the corner of house to the side door. It seemed to him he could hear her breathing inside. He gripped the door handle with both hands and pulled. It seemed very heavy and slow, and the door knob seemed unusually high, but he managed to open it and yellow light flooded out onto the stoop. He blinked and squinted, and when his eyes finally adjusted, he saw Sara Koepke, a young mother, bangs in her teary eyes, sitting on the kitchen counter, half-chopped fruit next to her bare hip, smooth naked thighs around Danny's waist, and her arms over his shoulders, wrists crossed behind his neck. Danny had shed his jean jacket but still wore his haystacker hat—also his Hawaiian shirt unbuttoned and baggy shorts dropped around his ankles. He stood on his tiptoes and did a regular little hop-hop while his round buttocks moved madly.

BEN WOKE LAUGHING IN HIS BED of twigs by the slough, by the river, by the road, and Sara Koepke stretched her long thin arm toward the sky and laid it across his chest.

'What's so funny?' she asked.

'Nothing.'

Despite his laughter, Ben didn't feel very good. He was hard and horny and unrested. He felt as if in order to imagine the ending he had to know when this trip began and he couldn't seem to remember.

Had it begun when he woke up one morning with his dead brother lying in the hallway?

Or the afternoon before, when he went to bed congratulating himself on finally coming home?

Or when he woke, the night before that, to see his mother's ghost in his bedroom. When he reread the letter. When he thought that, despite a mistake years ago, he could go home, forgive himself, bathe in brotherly love and make a start fresh.

Or perhaps it started when his parents died. Or when he first had Sara Koepke, his brother's girlfriend, on the grassy bank of the far pond on the day his grandfather died.

Or maybe he was trapped in Sara's dream.

Metaphysics was fatiguing. So was this burning need to love. His heart was too small, too brittle. Everything hurt. What else was new?

He shivered in a sudden blast of winter air—then suddenly his pores pricked open and he lay sweating in his nest of sticks. A spider web glistened in the tangle of branches above his head. This must be the journey Grandma had been talking about. Where he'd *see visions and dream dreams*. Where his *heart might open to the big world itself, or at least to his own sorrow and joy* . . .

Easy to say, he thought, and he tried to go back to sleep but the twigs were poking his side and his mind had begun to spin. He decided he'd start with what was clear, even to him. For one thing, it was indeed morning. August, he figured, as mist still clung to the surface of the slough water and the dew on the hillsides sparkled in pale yellow sunlight. For another, he and Sara Koepke blinked awake beneath the same box elder tree they'd gone to sleep under the night before. Which was a small good thing, he supposed. Normal, even. As was this troubled feeling he had. For how could he feel anything but troubled seeing—as he did now, for the first time since blinking awake—seeing Danny the Tuna lying still in the wagon, attracting flies along the length of his body?

'Shoo flies,' Ben said, and he stood to wave them away. But again they landed on Danny, and Ben slapped some of them. They smashed between his hand and Danny's fish face.

'Yuck,' Sara said, lifting her head.

Ben wiped his hand on the grass.

A car wound up the hollow and then across the flood plain from the river. At first they only heard it. Then they could see a dust plume approach. Finally the car appeared, grew larger, and larger, and then pulled to a stop next to them. It was a red convertible driven by a wind-blown granite-faced man with no neck, with black BB eyes and a large red mouth. In the bucket seat next to him sat a young blond woman, whose dark sunglasses emphasized and framed her tiny, turned-up nose. She wore a yellow sundress that did a similar thing with her breasts.

'You folks tell me where Frank Lloyd Wright is buried?'

Ben and Sara Koepke looked at each other.

'Who?' Sara said.

The blond woman caught sight (or whiff) of Danny the Tuna in the wagon. Her tiny nose made tiny wrinkles.

'Eeeew!' she said.

'The famous architect?' the man said. He smiled good-naturedly.

'Sorry,' Sara said, and shrugged. 'Never heard of him.'

The man pouted briefly, and then looked quizzically at the steering wheel in his hands. The blond woman kept her eyes on Danny the Fish in the wagon. She pursed her lips (the same color as the car).

'Sick,' she said.

The man ignored her—apparently he hadn't noticed Danny the Fish. 'I can't believe you two have never heard of Frank Lloyd Wright,' he said.

Ben shrugged. The blonde woman snorted. She kept her eyes on Danny and buzzed her window up.

'Let's put the top up, Randy,' she said.

Randy glanced quickly at the sky and smiled. 'It's a beautiful day!' Then to Ben, 'I'm a history buff.'

The blonde changed facial displays from Nauseated to Extremely Bored. She even took her eyes off Danny long enough to roll them.

'He was born with a blank time line in his head,' she said. 'Since then he's been filling in the dates. It's our honeymoon, but all we do is visit graves.'

'Your honeymoon!' Sara said. 'How romantic!'

Randy smiled sheepishly. 'It's been okay,' he said, 'but she's such a cunt whenever we're not doing *exactly* what she wants.'

'Don't let him fool you,' the blonde said confidentially to Sara. 'Plenty of times he has absolutely no problem with *exactly* what I want to do.'

Wanting to change the subject, Ben asked Randy, 'Any historic battles take place around here?'

'No biggies,' the man said. 'But mucho armies passed through.'

Ben pointed up the hollow toward the home farm. 'I've seen the Union army camped all along that hillside. Ten thousand little campfires. Rows and rows of tents.'

Randy was feeling his square chin, gazing up the hollow. He squinted. 'Wow,' he said. 'Really?'

'And I've seen a lot of bones,' Ben said. 'They stick out of our pasture down below where the army camped.'

'Gross!' the blonde said.

Randy glanced at her. Ben thought he was going to call her a cunt again but instead he lay his hand on her thigh and patted. 'What surprises a lot of people is that Genghis Khan came through here, too.'

'Really?' Ben said.

'Yup.' Randy gave a short breathy laugh, shook his head and finally looked away from the big field up the hollow where he'd been staring. 'Also Napoleon.'

'That does surprise me,' Ben said.

'This is Primo Tierra,' he explained, his voice expansive again, professorial, generous. 'Always was, always will be. There were a fair number of Indian massacres around here, too.'

'I've heard about them,' Ben said.

Randy cocked his head. Clicked his tongue. Glanced at the big old blue sky. 'Imagine it,' he said. 'The sun too blasted hot and the land too big, world without end . . . It must have driven their brains to reeling . . .'

'Whose?'

'Here we go again,' the blond woman said, rolling her eyes for Sara's benefit. 'History Hombre!'

'Numbed the pioneers with terror,' Randy continued. He whistled a brief descending note as if to emphasize his next point. 'A little native bloodshed with the Maxim gun must have been a reassuring thing.'

After that nobody spoke for a moment. A meadowlark whistled on a fence post. A hawk screeched. History Hombre turned to gaze up the hollow again, the thousand-yard stare. Sara broke the silence. 'Will you give us a ride to the sea? We can hook up the wagon to your back bumper.'

Randy snapped out of it. 'What wagon?'

She pointed at Danny the Tuna.

'Holy mole! What's that?'

The blond woman snorted and then gave Sara the *See-What-I-Have-To-Put-Up-With?* face.

Sara pointed at Ben. 'He caught it. He's such a good fisherman.'

'Yeah?' Randy was beaming. He sat up in his seat in order to get a better look. He focused his BB eyes, then unfocussed them. He shook his head slowly and clicked his tongue. 'Tuna?'

'Some fish, huh?' Sara Koepke said.

'We're trying to get it back to the sea,' Ben said.

History Hombre grinned broadly, still looking at the fish. 'I can't believe the size! As big as a man!'

'Why the sea?' the blonde asked.

'Catch and release,' Sara said.

Randy, still amazed and puzzled by the fish, turned to his wife. 'Did you see it before?'

'Yes.'

Randy looked stunned. 'Really?'

The blonde's brow creased quizzically. She fished in her purse for a nail file. Randy looked at Danny's fish body hanging over the sides of the wagon, the flies covering his side.

'Looks dead to me,' he said.

'Yeah,' Sara said. 'But we're hopeful.'

Ben lifted the handle of the red Radio Flyer and pulled it over behind the red convertible. As the big fish got close, the smell grew, and this time when the blonde said, 'Let's put the top up, honey,' Randy pushed a button and the car top emerged from its cocoon behind the back seat. Like a white wing, it unfolded into the air. Just as it had risen to the apex of its arch forward, it stopped.

'What's the problem?' the woman said.

'Stuck,' Randy said, and he turned and stepped over his seat onto the back seat and tried to pull the roof forward. It wouldn't budge. The fish smell was very strong now and lent urgency to the situation.

'Cripes,' Randy said. He stepped back into the front seat and sat down again behind the wheel.

'You giving up?' the woman said.

'There's nothing to do,' he said. 'It's done this before.'

He pushed the button that made the car roof retract, which it did, nicely.

Sara Koepke got into the back seat. Ben had tied the wagon handle to the back bumper with his shoestring, and then got in himself. He reached to take Sara's hand but she was using it to fan the air in front of her face.

'If we get moving,' she said, 'it won't smell so bad.'

So they did, and the car accelerated nicely around the curves. At the fork in the road on the way to the river, Randy asked which way and Sara told him left, although he could go right if he wanted, as both roads ended up at the sea eventually. But the left went straight and the right went over the top of the ridge and then down to the river that way, and so was used in the spring when the low road got too wet. Also by farmers with fields up there, and also by lovers—heaven knows, every couple in the valley has made out up there. Also (she took a breath) the Indians used it as a trail and there's a centuries-old campsite at the base of the hill. In fact the last Indians to be seen around here disappeared up that road to Mexico or to Canada—nobody knows where. Women, children, old people. Walked thousands and thousands of miles . . . all the way to wherever they went. Some say they followed that road all the way to The Other Side, if you catch my drift.

'Wow,' Randy said.

'Makes you damn grateful for cars, doesn't it?' Blondie said.

'Sure does,' History Hombre said, and he recounted a time he spent in Mongolia fishing for fish almost as big as this whopper they had on the wagon behind them, and how even the Mongols, great horsemen back in the old days, get around nowadays in SUVs and ATVs.

He drove slowly and steered around potholes that could upend the wagon dragging behind. The forward motion kept the breeze fresh, but Danny had been dead too long now and his odor spread in a wake behind the wagon and began to attract coyotes. Coming from every direction, led onward by the excitement of something putrid, coyotes emerged from the brush and forest, dipped into the borrow pits and up again onto the road, and loped behind and alongside the wagon. The boldest of the pack moved in for a quick lick, a sneaky little bite on Danny's tail.

An alert Ben noticed first. 'Hey!' he shouted.

'What?'

'Faster!' Ben said, and Randy stepped on the gas and the car accelerated, and the wagon did too. But not Danny. Danny bounced onto the road and was quickly surrounded by coyotes.

'Stop!'

Randy did, and Ben jumped out of the car. He shouted '*Back, beasts!*' and chased the coyotes off with a stick. Then he carefully lifted his brother back into the wagon, centered him, and climbed back into the car.

Randy started driving again, but again the coyotes followed the wagon, and again he had to drive too fast, and again Danny flopped out of the wagon and was surrounded.

Ben hopped out of the car and chased the coyotes off. He lifted his brother and put him back into the wagon. He used his hand to wipe the dirt and gravel off his brother's side. He centered him on the wagon and then climbed back in the car, but this time Blondie said, 'Eeeew, gross, you smell!' And even Sara Koepke stayed on the far end of the backseat.

The third time Danny fell out of the wagon, Ben lifted him back on, and then sat on top of him, straddling him. He felt bad that Danny had lost scales with each fall, and his dorsal fin had come unglued, and the coyotes had managed to take a couple of chunks out of his tail. So he held on to the wagon handle with one hand, and to a golf club he found in the ditch with the other, and he called up to Randy to begin driving. The car pulled them slowly down the road. Ben leaned forward over Danny for balance, his face close to Danny's face. He took a good long look at Danny's fish eye and Danny's fish face and he smelled the smell of decaying fish, and he remembered Danny sitting on top of him like this when they were boys, burping into his nose and asking, 'Can you smell that? Can you? This is a nose test!'

He felt Danny's body shift under him, and he turned in time to see a yellow coyote tugging on Danny's tail. He swung the club back and bonked the coyote on the nose, and it snarled and backed off, but another was there, and then another. Sneaky coyotes, wild coyotes, coyotes abandoned by Indians and tourists.

Good god, Ben thought, there are hundreds!

He held on and fought back his nausea, from the car exhaust, too, and even though he suspected by now that this journey was outside of time and space, he wished the sea weren't so far away and the road weren't so bad. And also he wished he had a watch or a calendar, because ever since leaving his office in our nation's capital, ever since leaving his house, ever since getting off the jet plane and driving back home, turning off the main highway and winding into the hills, he'd lost track of time. Perhaps he should have paid closer attention when on the day of his arrival it had been summer at the airport, yet during the course of an hour's drive to the home farm, after turning off the main highway and winding back into the hills, the sumac had turned crimson on the side of the road and the birch leaves gold as coins.

But even if he'd been suspicious, what could he have done? He knew it would be weird to come home again. He just didn't know how weird. Still he hung on. The seasons change and a man's got to live with the changes. He's got to bear up and think straight. He can't lose his mind just because things get weird. He didn't think he was as blissfully ignorant as his grandma had suggested. Twenty-five years ago he'd made a major change in his life. He'd left this farm and a disastrous affair and built a pretty good life. A life others envied. Yet as neat and clean as it seemed on the surface, his mother's ghost had still come haunting. *Your brother forgives you*, she'd said. *Don't waste that.*

And then his grandma: *It's about doing, loving . . . the whole mess of it . . . only then should you think.*

Think what?

More bumps, and there was nothing to do but hold on to the wagon and to his brother. He could hear Sara's story-telling voice in the car ahead, hear it pause, hear laughter. He wondered what she was saying, wondered if she was telling intimate things about them, about him. Maybe she was saying that the big fish was really her dead husband, and Ben had killed him and then had ravished her in the grass after twenty-five years away—and boy, what a letdown!

Ben thought he heard Blondie's knowing cackle, and he turned and whacked another coyote square in the nose with all his might. It cried and dropped back, but another immediately lunged for Danny's tail. Ben whacked this one too. It let go but didn't fall back.

They hadn't even made love. Or maybe they had? A long time ago before he left. Of course they had. Things happened and then they were past and you either remembered or you didn't. But if you didn't, did that mean they never happened? Forget the past, Grandma had said, and the dead die twice. But still, people *do* forget. Things *are* forgotten. And when they are, who is to say they actually happened? God? But God doesn't talk. He keeps his mouth shut, mostly. You have to stay still, maybe, and listen. And if you don't hear God, you might hear the mysterious screams. From the bone cave or from the Screaming Woman. His grandma told him both of those stories. Or perhaps he dreamed them. For years Ben had dreamed over and over again that he and Sara

Koepke were alone in the hay mow, gold fingers of sunshine streaking through the siding, and he reached to embrace her and she turned to sawdust in his arms . . .

That had been his dream. Or maybe it really happened? He couldn't remember anymore, and it didn't seem to matter, as the coyotes were getting bolder now and moving in to bite Danny, even as Ben flailed madly at them with the club. The undersides of the clouds had turned orange with dusk, and then crimson. How far was it, he wondered, to the sea?

Darkness settled and he heard the coyotes running alongside him, felt their breathing, but he couldn't see them anymore. Both his hands ached terribly. The one holding the club had cramped, and he had to relax it, to open it, to let the coyotes move in for a couple of bites while he rested. In the car ahead, he could hear laughter and music, and he saw the stars above, and his arms and legs felt so tired he couldn't control them anymore. He was hungry and thirsty and he shook his cramped hand to loosen it. He could feel his brother's fish body between his legs, and he could feel the coyotes pulling at it so he grabbed the club again and swung wildly. He didn't know if he hit one or not. He couldn't feel his hand or his arm or his shoulder anymore, and he wondered, briefly, if the great Tiger Woods ever had to straddle a giant fish on a wagon behind a car, breathing exhaust and his brother's decomposing body while beating off coyotes with a three-wood.

Then the club flew out of his hand and he could feel the coyotes move in closer, thicker, and he could smell their breath in the dark, feel their muzzles next to his thighs as they planted their fangs into the big fish and pulled.

Ben closed his eyes and hung on, but even with his eyes closed he could see the chunks of white meat glowing in the dark before blinking out, disappearing down each gullet. Oh! He heard Sara's loud story-telling voice and again he wondered how far to the sea. The road followed the river and he strained to see across it to the green light at Daisy's Riverside Bar and Grill. Danny and Sara had been married there and, late after the reception, even joined some of their more dedicated guests in a skinny-dip. Ben had swum out in the river listening to the music and voices on the pier, and Sara, wearing only her veil, appeared next to him in the water and slipped around behind, wrapped her arms around his shoulders and sent shivers down his spine with the words, *Oh, Ben. I love him, too.*

The sand gave way under his feet and he kicked in the sudden depths. Before he could turn, she'd swum off toward shore. Ben tried to keep up but had drifted into a stronger current, so could only watch as her white veil like a jellyfish on the black water moved gradually away from him, back toward the pier, toward the green light and the music and laughter, and the dark fields of the continent rolling on endlessly into the night.

From the Radio Flyer wagon Ben could see the red taillights on the car ahead. He wrapped his exhausted limbs around his fish brother, feeling not so much terror at how his brother's putrid body was yanked and yanked again by feeding coyotes, but despair at how what seemed so close that night (and for many nights before), could have slipped so easily from his grasp.

While Sara Koepke walked naked out of the water and down the beach, gathered and slipped on a robe to join her husband and the rest of the party, Ben swam on against the current, stretching toward tomorrow but borne back ceaselessly into the past.

RAIN FELL IN BIG FAT DROPS on the fields and waters and forests of the world, and it splattered on Ben's face, too, and woke him. He opened his eyes and noticed the night had turned to day and instead of the green light on the river, he saw a line of yellow fluorescent lights, and then the cloudy sky disappeared entirely under a white metal roof that made the rain sound like a burst of applause.

Now what?

He lay still for a moment and took his bearings. Instead of lying on his stomach in a wagon, he lay on his back across the buttery leather backseat of the convertible. And instead of his head lying on his brother's cold and putrid face, it lay across gray-haired Sara Koepke's warm and fragrant lap.

'You have a nice sleep, sweetie?' she asked. She stroked his hair and he sat up, blinked and looked past History Hombre and Blondie in the front seat, through the windshield at a wooden menu hanging over an orange picnic table crowded with teenagers.

Beyond that, more yellow fluorescent lights rimmed the big roof from which water poured in gray cascades that made it hard to see even a block down the road.

'You all right?' Sara asked.

Ben knew this drive-in. He'd worked here. Sara had worked here. Danny before them had worked here, too.

'Yeah, I guess,' he said, and he looked back over the convertible trunk to the Radio Flyer wagon, which extended out from under the roof into the rain. Danny the Fish seemed to be changing again. For one thing, he looked freshly caught and gorgeous. Neither rotten nor coyote-bitten. Blue and yellow and pink stripes had emerged on his side, shiny and clean. Eyes soft and bright. He even moved his gills slightly, or seemed to, as the rainwater washed over him and filled the wagon.

'I had a bad dream,' he said.

She smiled, brushed his cheek with the back of her hand.

He swallowed. His mouth was dry. 'I thought we were going to the sea,' he said.

But the sound of the rain on the metal roof was suddenly deafening.

'What?' She pointed to her ears.

He repeated himself.

'We thought we'd stop and get a bite to eat first!' she yelled.

The rain let up slightly, and the noise on the metal roof quieted. Ben studied the menu. At least that was predictable and familiar. Burgers with a choice of nine toppings. Curly fries or jumbo fries or home fries. Shakes in three flavors, sodas in six. He felt hungry and distracted himself by deciding what to order. Mmmm. His mouth watered. Suddenly he could hardly wait to eat. So when Blondie turned around in the front seat and Ben could see she'd changed, become somebody new, he barely flinched.

'Tami?' he said.

She smiled. The last time he'd seen her was years ago in the hay mow of the horse stables where he and Danny had been baling hay. A teenager. Now she was a woman, and she wore an expensive coral necklace, a taupe velvet blouse and matching slacks. Her hands were set off with bracelets of pearls white as curdled milk, gold rings on her fingers. Her hair looked like spun silver. And despite her having aged quite a bit, a good thirty years Ben guessed, judging by her face, the wrinkles under her chin and around her mouth and eyes, she still had a figure like a palm tree loaded with dates.

'Wow,' he said. 'You look wonderful.'

'Good morning,' she said, and she and Sara gave each other a look. Ben blushed and he didn't know why. He glanced away at the History Hombre standing behind the car now, just inside the overhang, peering through the falling rain at the wagon and the big fish. He looked different, too, yet familiar. No longer History Hombre, he was much bigger and he had jet black hair instead of thinning yellow. A darker complexion. And instead of casual clothes, he wore a lovely yellow pinpoint oxford shirt and a burgundy tie under an expensive blue suit.

'Harold Little Boy?' Ben said.

'Thought you'd never wake up,' Harold said. He stepped forward to shake Ben's hand and Ben saw the unmistakable way those familiar eyes narrowed when he grinned. Still handsome, but age had given him the beginnings of jowls. Also a gold watch and large pinkie ring. Ben tried not to stare. In the old days when they'd worked together, Harold Little Boy had worn his hair in a long black ponytail. He had a collection of wild-colored headbands, smocks, and leggings. Even when he drove the tractor or stacked hay, he wore moccasins.

'You've changed,' Ben said.

Harold Little Boy laughed. He looked at Danny, beautiful and large in the wagon. 'That's a nice fish,' he said. 'Real pretty. Sara tells me you caught it.'

Ben shrugged.

'I don't even remember you picking us up,' Ben said. 'I've been in the back having some serious dreams.'

'Dreams?' Harold closed his eyes and lifted his chin—an imitation of himself many years ago, how he used to pretend to interpret Danny's and Ben's dreams. *'Were there dogs fucking?'*

'What?'

'And were they fucking in the sunshine or shadow?'

'I—'

'Did you see a little girl? Was she watching the dogs fuck? Or was she turned sideways? Was she wearing shoes?'

They both laughed.

'We saw you and Sara on the side of the road,' Harold said. 'Me and Tami—you recognized her, didn't you? We live on the coast now. We're back on vacation, a little nostalgic tour.'

'You guys married?'

'Twenty-two years!' Harold Little Boy grinned. 'We own a construction business—we build highways.'

Ben noticed his teeth had been straightened and whitened. He looked good.

Harold patted his stomach. 'Let's eat, okay?'

One of the teenage boys sitting at the orange picnic table had noticed Danny the Fish in the wagon, and he walked over to take a look. Another followed. Then another. Also some of the kitchen staff. They wore white aprons and white paper hats and they joined the crowd looking through the rain at Danny in the wagon.

What kind of fish? they asked. How did you catch it? What are you doing with it? Is it a world record?

Ben made up answers as fast as he could. He felt bothered by the boys' interest, though. He felt vaguely guilty. His heart beat faster.

'Haven't you ever seen a big fish in a wagon before?'

Suddenly hangdog, the boys looked one last time at Danny the Fish and then they shuffled back to the picnic table and the kitchen.

A waitress came out to take their order. When she left, Ben said to Sara, 'Don't you think he looks different from the way he used to look?' He was talking about Danny the Fish, no longer exactly a tuna, but longer and thinner, whiter, bluer. A marlin? Harold Little Boy heard and thought Ben was talking about him again, about his changes, so he answered, 'Haven't we all?'

'What?' Ben said.

Harold wrinkled his forehead and made a contemplative face. 'I mean, even beyond biology, don't we all have a great joyous need to change? To become someone new?'

Ben shrugged. 'I was just—'

'When I lived here,' Harold interrupted. 'I was all into being an *Indian*. I was angry, and that was normal after what my ancestors suffered here. But with the kind of anger I felt, there are two fates—either you go to prison or you get over it. I guess I did the second, only it was more like a long fall than a willful climb. I bounced around and ended up on the West Coast, and for a while I was all into being a *Native American*. It helped me build the business, get contracts. Then I had a mini-crisis and decided I'd been neglecting half my heritage. I've got almost as much Scots-Irish blood as I do Cree, after all. But that got weird, too, every other day wondering what I was supposed to think or do according to *my heritage*. So I gave up the notions of *blood* and *tribe* and decided that just being a *man* was hard enough. That's what freedom is, right?'

Ben didn't know what to say. They were sitting back in the car now, waiting for their food.

'The capacity to change,' Harold said. 'The freedom to change. That's what this country gives its citizens, right?'

'I guess so,' Ben said. He was confused by the conversation, though. He was watching the waitress load the tray with their food, get set for delivery. His mouth was watering.

'Yet here's the funny thing,' Harold was saying. 'No matter how many times we change, we always carry a sense that our true self was lost a long time ago. This is our national affliction. When I was young, I thought it was only an Indian affliction but it's not. The whole goddam country suffers from it. We change our name, our face, our body, our credentials, our jobs, our homes. We change our stories about ourselves. We change whatever the hell we want to change, because that's freedom—but we can't change the way all of that change makes us feel. The sadness. The sense of loss and the urgency to fill that hole with sentimental dream-come-true shit. It doesn't go away—and the longing deep inside never changes, either. You know what I'm saying?'

Nobody answered him because the waitress was delivering the food. She hung the tray on the driver's side window. Harold Little Boy distributed the food as he talked.

'We long to wake up one day speaking the old mother tongue,' he said. 'We long to wake up in a little shack with a turf fire, or a tepee with a twig fire, and all of our lost family will be there, surrounding us, and they won't be stealing from each other or slitting each other's throats. It'll be like on TV commercials, all happy smiles, a warm welcome in Gaelic or Hausa or Lao or Cherokee or . . .'

Everybody ate burgers and fries, and sipped milkshakes through straws. Afterward, Tami and Sara Koepke disappeared into the bathroom and Ben hopped out of the car and stood leaning back against the trunk, looking at his brother in the wagon. The rain had slowed to a drizzle, and the noise on the big roof was quietly comforting. Harold Little Boy followed him back behind the car and was still talking about who-knows-what. Ben stared thoughtfully at Danny's new streamlined shape, his blue beauty, and his nose stretching into a sword. He tried to remember killing his brother but could only remember lying down in his old bedroom and going to sleep thinking about Sara's face—her crazy face, her wounded face, her happy face. He glanced at her now, with Tami, back from the bathroom and into the car again, using this moment to stretch their necks toward the rearview and touch up their lipstick. They'd changed clothes, too. Sara now wore shorts and a t-shirt. She'd cut her hair. She looked younger. She turned. Yes. She was a teenager. She had a line of pimples on her forehead. She noticed Ben looking at her and she smiled, blushed? Harold Little Boy continued talking, and Ben nodded, but he looked back again at Danny on the wagon and thought of the living, breathing Danny, standing in the stairwell with a hammer and describing how he'd put out rat poison, and that a dead rat was the source of the terrible smell. The rat that had already been dead for days when Ben arrived back home that first afternoon. The decomposing rat smell had been the smell Sara Koepke referred to when she'd showed him to his old room and he'd asked if he could take a nap. It was the smell she kept talking about during that pathetically under-cooked chicken dinner, too. Or was that the last night he'd been home, twenty-five years ago? The final night before he'd gone away?

He remembered drifting to sleep listening to Danny tapping the plaster to find the dead rodent. Then hearing Danny and Sara making love in the hallway twenty-five years ago on the morning of the day before he'd finally left home. His grandma had taught him how long sounds last, how far they carry, so what surprised him most was how hearing it again made him feel. He'd come home with the vague hope that desire might have faded with age and distance and he'd be able to forgive himself easily, the way an adult can forgive himself for stealing chocolate from Grandpa's candy bowl when he was a child. But instead, Ben's desire for Sara seemed to have grown. Or else Ben had simply forgotten how possessed he'd been. He remembered that long afternoon, years ago, sitting in his bedroom with a pistol on his lap. And the familiar visitor who saved him. And his madman marathon hitchhike to the coast and up north to Alaska. Then out into the gulf to fish halibut, and the next winter up in the Bering for crab. He'd survived and made a killing. Or as Skipper said, *He'd killed and made a surviving.* And when he'd had enough, when the nights of mad work on mad seas started to scare him, he flew back across the country to the East Coast for college, studied mechanical engineering and found work on the Project, a system of un-built lasers meant to protect the continent against the unknown and unknowable and unimaginable. An imagined shield of lovely lapis beams that might never be completed, but whose imagined purpose (safety and security forever) gave him the means to live his version of a good life. Good work for good money, living in a good house. Having good friends. Reading good books and eating good food. Having good sex with a good many good women.

And in all of that distraction, he'd simply forgotten how he used to lie awake night after night wanting her, until even the notion of *wanting her* had begun to see seem quaintly romantic and untrue.

Now here he was, a fifty-year-old man, knowing to the depths of his every living cell that he was going to die. And that he had only this one life—no others lined up and ready to go—this one heart, and after all these years the grand effect of all of his strivings and distractions had been . . . had meant . . . *what?*

The rain stopped suddenly. No more drizzle on the big metal roof of the drive-in and the air smelled clean and the food tasted good. Ben looked at Danny the Fish lying wet in the wagon behind the car. He'd grown a long sword and was clearly now a blue marlin. Harold Little Boy had gone to the men's room, and

Sara Koepke and Tami sat in the front seat, talking about some place they used to go years ago, a cave. Did Sara remember it?

'How could I forget?' she said. 'None of us will ever forget the bone cave!'

Tami said she sure remembered some wild times there, all right, and what a shame Danny had to be out of town because it'd be great to go there again and party like rock stars.

A suddenly older Sara Koepke reached across the back seat and touched Ben's arm. She was his age again, a half century. She'd been rubbing lotion on her freckled hands and her touch was cool. 'Let's pick up some beer and go there,' she said.

'But—'

'I know it's a delay. We'll get Danny to the sea. But for now, please? Please please please?'

Before Ben could answer, he noticed a man with a brown bowler and a tweed jacket get out of an old black Model T Ford in the parking lot behind the car. The man rubbed his palms together briskly and walked over to the wagon and stood looking down at Danny the Marlin.

'That's a fine fish,' he said, his Scottish accent so thick Ben could barely understand him. 'You're indeed the catch*air*?'

Ben nodded.

'May I see *yurre* permit?'

'My what?' he asked.

'Permit, laddie. I'd appreciate a wee look.'

He had the same face as the black-hatted lawman, but his voice was different and his eyes clear. 'You can see?'

The man pulled his tweed sport coat back, revealing a pistol in a shoulder strap. 'I'm the gamekeeper,' he said, and winked, sending an icy chill down Ben's spine. 'And 'tis to your great misfortune that what I see is an illegal fish.'

BEN PRESSED HIS NOSE TO THE SCREEN in the living room window. He had to stand on his tiptoes. Flies buzzed around his face yet he dared not turn away. In the yard he watched his grandpa as a little boy following a lipless old man from wagon to barn, from barn to wagon. They hitched the horses. They loaded the tools. Including dynamite. Grandpa's hair lay flat, sandy colored, a cowlick above his forehead. He wore overalls with one strap, old boots. No shirt. Great-grandpa Clarence wore a straw hat, flannel shirt, overalls, and boots.

'Are they ghosts?' Ben asked.

His grandma, behind him, said, 'They are going up to the ridge to blast out stumps. They made that field. They cut the wood and blew up the stumps, pulled the roots to the edge of the forest with the team. They worked hard. It took them ten years. It's what they did, blast and pull stumps.'

'Didn't they also kill Indians?'

'Yes, they did that, too. Or Clarence did. But you can kill people a lot quicker than you can kill and remove three-hundred-year-old oak trees.'

Great-grandpa Clarence climbed on the wagon, and took the reins in his hands, and Grandpa climbed in the back and sat on the tools. Great-grandpa clicked his tongue and the two massive horses began moving together, pulling the wagon back behind the house, lifting a trail of dust that followed them down the hollow and out of sight.

'You have to remember,' his grandma was saying, 'how every day we woke and the sun shone or it didn't. We looked out these same windows. We felt hungry and tired and happy and miserable. We rested our sore backs. We cried tears of grief. We had what we had because we did the work necessary. We built this house, our home and that barn and those sheds. We took the stone from the quarry. We carried it here on our backs, or in wagons drawn by beasts, and we grew the food to feed ourselves and our beasts, and we made the clothes we wore to protect us from the cold and the rain.

'We prayed for rain and we prayed that our children, your mother and her sister and brother would not get sick and die, but we never prayed that our little Annie, your mother's big sister, wouldn't fall off the porch and land on her head and die, and we never prayed that your mother wouldn't drown like she drowned with your father. And I think of her, in the car, with the windows up, as it submerged in the black water, and I wake at night screaming, or I'm falling like little Annie—she was only three, you know. I can still see her big brown eyes and how they must have looked just before she fell, as she fell. I see what she saw with her eyes, the flagstone coming at me and when I hit, I wake, unhappy, of course.'

Flies buzzed around Ben's face. He could hear them on the screen. He could hear his grandma's voice . . . 'See?'

'What, Grandma?'

'You'll thank me, boy.'

Ben did not know what to say. The vision of his grandpa and great-grandpa on the wagon had turned into the memory of his grandpa and Danny as a boy on the wagon hitched up to the team, Billy and Burt, two gray geldings. It was an old hobby of his grandpa's to take out the buckboard and the team from time to time.

With his nose pressed against the window screen, Ben was crying.

'Why are you crying, boy?'

'Because Grandpa never takes me. He always takes Danny. Why doesn't he take me?'

Grandma cackled, and the sound of it raised the hair on the back of his neck. 'Close up your heart with self-pity and you may as well poke out your eyes.'

'I'm afraid,' he said.

She lay her hand on his shoulder. 'Don't be. If the ghosts wanted to hurt you, they would have hurt you long ago.'

Flies buzzed on the screen near his face. 'Where do the flies come from, Grandma?'

'The woodwork,' she said. 'Every day a hundred more are born. They cluster on the window, and they do their little thing, and they lay more eggs in the woodwork, and they die.'

'Every day Danny and I kill them,' he said.

She stayed quiet.

'Where is Danny, Grandma?'

'He's back at the ponds fishing with Grandpa.'

'When are they coming back?'

'Soon,' she said.

His nose pressed against the screen, he watched the day darken, the pasture and the hills turning black, the sky pastel pink and yellow, then pale silver, indigo, midnight blue.

'Grandma?'

'Yes?'

'Can I take my nose away from the screen now?'

'Not until you see some more ghosts for me.'

Ben closed his eyes. 'Okay,' he said. 'I see Gramps when he was little. He keeps crossing the lawn with tools and stuff, putting them in the grass.'

'What's he doing?' she asked.

'It's hard to see.'

'Try,' she said.

Ben squeezed his eyes closed tight and kept them that way. He could see light green and dark red splotches.

'He's working in the yard. By the fence.'

'Yes,' she said. 'Which one?'

'The one around the yard.'

'What's he doing?'

'He's taking the decorations off the fence posts and digging a hole and burying the decorations.'

'Yes,' she said. 'Can you see the decorations?'

'No,' he said.

'Look harder.'

He tried. They were white balls.

'Where is the hole?' she asked.

'Here in the yard.'

'Close?'

'Yes.'

'Then look harder.'

He pressed his nose harder against the screen. He closed his eyes tighter. 'Skulls,' he said.

'The *decorations*?'

'Yes. Grandpa is throwing them into the new hole he dug.'

'Grandpa doesn't like them.'

'No,' Ben said. 'Why?'

'Because they are cursed,' she said.

Ben felt frightened by the way his grandmother said that word, *cursed*. He swallowed. 'Grandma?'

'Yes?'

'Can you see any ghosts?' His nose was still pressed against the screen. He could smell ripe grasses. He could smell chamomile and cow manure.

'Of course I can,' she said. 'But you need to, too. Do you feel that?'

'What?'

'That.'

'Oh!' He felt a cool breeze on his neck. 'That's you blowing, Grandma.'

'No,' Grandma said, 'that's a ghost passing. In my bones I can feel your mother running around like she used to run around as a girl. Her skinny little body, her face like a fawn. She loved your father.'

'She forgave him. Danny told me.'

'She forgave herself.'

'For what?'

Grandma's voice sounded sad. 'Close your eyes,' she said.

Ben had never opened them but he didn't tell her that. He kept them closed and his nose pressed to the screen. He heard his grandfather digging, the shovel striking a rock. He heard cows bawling down the pasture. He heard the bull roar and it scared him. He braced himself for his grandmother's voice, but when it came, she was humming a hymn from church. No words. Only her voice, and her voice wavered. It was clear as a bell, and then it faded, and he had to strain to be sure she was still behind him. Then the voice grew loud again. She began to speak in a different voice, an unfamiliar language. He kept his eyes closed, afraid to turn around.

'Two white women had been killed, you know,' she said. 'The last straw, and that's what encouraged the open hunting of natives. A lone brave here. Three or four there. A small gathering attending an autumn festival gunned down like buffalo. Quite a number of settlers tried to save the Indians, to feed them, to stop the massacres, but not enough. The anti-vigilantes were outnumbered. So federal troops were sent for, and arrived, and they camped across the creek there. A hasty plan was made to evacuate all the Indians to a reservation a hundred and thirty miles away at Walleye Lake. Word went out. The last living Indians gathered in the valley here. They were ragged and starving, and the army was not prepared to feed them, so they started dying even before the march began. They say four hundred and fifty souls headed down the hollow toward the river, took the ridge road, and disappeared forever from this country. Only a handful ever arrived at the reservation, and most of them died soon after. Seems there were no provisions there, either.'

Ben heard the breeze rustle the leaves of the ash tree, and he heard his grandfather digging, and he heard the bull roar again. Behind him, he felt the wind on his neck, his grandmother's breath.

'Listen,' she said. 'A group of Indians, my mother's family among them, didn't gather here before the march to Walleye Lake. They hung back. They tried to hide. Women and children mostly.

Your grandpa wouldn't talk about it if they put him on the rack and stretched him. Or maybe he would, I don't know. But you should know how it was.'

'*Stoooooppppp!*' Ben yelled. He was tired of her lectures and speeches and gruesome stories, and tired of standing tiptoe with his nose against the screen. He turned and ran past her through the living room and into the kitchen, across the polished maple floor and out the back door and into the yard. The sun had fallen, disappeared. The stars lit the night sky. He ran into the pasture and kept going until he came to a stream. On the far side, he could see the shadows of two women bathing with Coyote. He stood still and listened to the peepers in the dark, and crickets, and the two women laughing and splashing in the water. He felt a young man's strength in his legs and shoulders. He felt the urge to howl like a wolf so he did and he watched Coyote run away up the hill.

'Hey Big Wolf,' one of the women called from the other side of the water. 'Come over here!'

Ben crossed the stream. Now it was a river. He had to swim hard to get to the other side. He arrived wet and cold. He noticed the two women were naked and immediately he began to fondle their breasts.

'What are you doing?' they asked.

'Trying to see which I like the best,' he said. He was serious but the two women only laughed. He finally picked one and knelt down and began nursing her sweet milk. He laid his head in her lap and she picked lice out of his hair. His penis grew hard and he stopped nursing and rolled the woman over onto her knees and he tried to mount her but the other woman laughed and pulled him off and scolded him for being so naughty. The other woman was Sara Koepke, and he didn't know why he hadn't recognized her before. She pulled him down into a bed of grass and they lay together and she touched him and he touched her back.

'You shouldn't,' she said. 'I'm menstruating.'

'I like blood,' he said.

He slid down her body and even in starlight he could see the blood on her belly and thighs, and he sat up, and he could see the blood on his hands and arms and chest and—

She scrambled out from under him. 'Help!' she said, giggling and running away. 'A vampire!'

He struggled to stand but found himself alone and naked, his hair full of cockleburs. Also his thighs were stuck together with semen. He managed to hop into the stream to bathe, and he used his knife to cut the burrs from his hair. Then he walked back to the farmhouse. He saw his grandma hanging laundry in the yard and felt guilty for running away, and so he lied again and said he heard they found her dead, her and Danny dead, and so that's why he'd cut his hair, and now he was so happy she was alive. He believed his lie so completely that he burst into tears.

Grandma wasn't fooled. 'You heard I was dead?' she said, and cackled. 'Me and Danny? I guess you heard wrong.'

'Thank the Lord!' Ben said. He had his head down, face covered with his hands, sobbing.

'Cuss the Lord,' he heard her say, 'for your grandfather passed on last night. We looked for you as soon as we found him but you was out tomcatting with your brother's girlfriend—'

Ben dropped to his knees, lay his face in the grass, his cheek against the sharp edge of a bone pushing up through the soil.

'My baaaaaaby!' his grandmother screamed, shrieking, howling until the word had disintegrated into pure sound that lifted Ben off the ground and filled him with terror. Or was that Danny actually lifting him up, carrying him down the hollow toward the white house and red barn on the day they learned their parents had died? On the day Ben broke his leg jumping out of a tree? It might have been—certainly could have been—but it didn't matter. What did was how the scream crossed the valley like a scarlet wave and bounced off the green hillside up the hollow and disappeared into the forest, raced over the prairie, rolled over mountain ranges and distant seas. What did was how the scream traveled around the world and back again, a wail of grief that sent shivers up the spine of anyone who heard it pass, masters and slaves, gypsies, tourists, Chinese acrobats, sailors on the sea, camel riders in caravans, men pulling handcarts in crowded cities, waitresses on smoke breaks, women carrying water on their heads, lovers parting to gaze inward at the wall, wandering salesmen, jungle tribesmen, corporate pirates in their corner offices. They all heard the passing scream just as Ben had, mysterious and disembodied, and each and every listener filled for a moment with a cold and terrible dread.

DUSK FELL AND THEY RESTED on a rock, caught their breath, the three boys. A black web of crooked oak branches held the pewter sky. It was fall but the air smelled of swamp and Indian summer and the cured hay bales they'd hauled from the truck along the narrow path that followed the slough to the sandstone bluffs, then up the trail most of the way to the cave.

'Call me Big Hay Fella,' Harold said, and they laughed, and Harold spread his four fingers, the index coupled with the middle, the pinkie coupled with the ring. They looked like two legs. He lifted his hand to his nose and sniffed where the two legs met. He rolled his head back.

'How 'bout it, Benji?'

'Gross.'

Danny shook his head. 'If you think it's gross, you'll never get any.'

'Maybe I don't want any.'

'Oh, yes you do,' Harold said, snorting, snorting again. 'Oh yes you do!'

They lifted the bales the rest of the way, struggling with them up the rocks and over the ledge. They set the bales at the entrance, the porch. They broke one apart in the living room, in the big wide part of the cave about fifteen feet back from the entrance, and they broke another even farther back, in the part of the cave they called the bedroom. Just past there, in a slight narrowing of the cave, were the bones, but the boys didn't go that far back.

Then they each opened a bottle of warm beer. They sat on the porch hay bale and waited. It was dark. A whippoorwill called. They had a flashlight but they didn't turn it on. They had matches and wood but they didn't start a fire. They watched the stars and they listened to a barred owl. Harold Little Boy could talk to the owls. Danny and Ben could too, but the owls actually talked back to Harold.

'Think they chickened out?'

'Nope,' Harold said.

Each finished a couple of beers. Even Ben, who had to hold his nose. After the second, he started whooping and running around in circles in the dark cave. He held his arms out in front of him so he wouldn't run into the wall. He could hear Danny and Harold laugh. The exertion felt good and he wasn't nervous anymore. He was sweating and out of breath and that's when he saw the yellow flashlight down below in the woods, the beam dancing this way and that.

'Shhhhh,' Danny said, and grabbed him.

Tami and Sara Koepke appeared as shadows behind their flashlight on the trail below. Ben watched them get closer. He could hear them talking and then the sound of their feet on the rock as they climbed up the last few feet and stood breathing hard.

'Turn the light off,' Harold said.

The switch clicked on the metal flashlight body and the beam went dark.

'Any beer left?' It was Tami. Danny got her a bottle, also one for Sara Koepke.

'Wow,' Tami said.

Both girls tilted their beer bottles back and drank fast. Tami held her nose like Ben did. Danny went over to stand next to Sara Koepke, and when she finished a long drink, he took her arm and pulled her back into the cave. Ben noticed how he didn't even speak. Nor did she. After they were gone, Tami took another drink of beer and Harold and she disappeared.

Ben sat alone on the hay bale. His stomach was turning circles and he wanted to shit. He couldn't see anything back in the cave because it was too dark but he could hear kissing and soft breathing. He told himself he didn't care what happened. He was curious, of course, and he didn't want to be a chicken, but he knew if nothing happened that was okay too. He just didn't want to miss something great. He thought about Tami and he knew she was the one, if either of them would. She was the one who would do it with him. But something about her face, the petty little twist she made with her mouth sometimes when she was irritated, scared him. He would much prefer Sara Koepke, whom he'd known for as long as he'd known anybody, but then again, it seemed weird to do it the first time with somebody you knew so well. He thought about kissing her, about touching her neck where her hair falls, and he thought about her legs, smooth and beautiful and . . . he could never think about any of the rest. He couldn't imagine her doing it with Danny. He couldn't imagine anybody doing it without embarrassment.

Harold Little Boy touched Ben's arm. 'Here,' he said.

'What?'

Harold laughed. 'She likes you!'

It was dark so all Ben could see were the stars and the shadows behind him in the cave, and he felt Harold's hand on his wrist, then his hand, and he felt his hand lifted and then his hand in Tami's hand. She pulled him to his feet and he was going to say something but then remembered how Danny hadn't said anything, nor had Sara Koepke, and so he knew he didn't have to. She was a hand in the dark, nothing more. He stood and walked back and heard Harold Little Boy open a beer bottle and settle comfortably on the hay bale.

Ben and Tami lay down on the hay. He couldn't quite catch his breath. He was afraid Tami was naked and he didn't know what to do with his hands. She embraced him, kissed his face, and he felt her body against his, and she had her clothes on so he relaxed a little bit. He put his arm under her head.

'There,' she said.

She kissed him on the mouth and he kissed her back. He'd never kissed a girl like that before and was surprised at how pleasant it was, the explosion of taste and texture. He didn't know what to do with his hands while he kissed her so he slipped one of them into her jeans without unbuttoning the waistband, and she pulled her mouth back from his and said, 'Oh!' slightly startled. But she didn't stop him. She kissed him again, and while they were kissing he pushed his hand down farther but her jeans were tight and the angle was bad. He could feel her pubic hair and he'd never touched a girl there, so for a moment had to stop kissing her because his chest wouldn't expand enough for him to inhale sufficient air. He felt as if he were drowning and the waistband of her jeans was keeping the blood from getting to his hand.

He adjusted the angle to take some of the pressure off his wrist, and he pushed his hand farther down her pants and began to move it up and down, feel her press against him, up and down. He pushed his hand even farther, and finally found her furrow, and he pressed his finger there, and felt for a hole. He pulled up again wondering if he'd missed it somewhere higher, then pushed down again, searching, and down farther, way down, past where he thought it would be, then up again, pushing hard, then even father down until – 'Oh,' he said, because suddenly, surprisingly, his finger felt swallowed inside her. How amazing—so sudden and wet! He felt momentarily comfortable with his hand like that, and his other around her shoulders, and both of her hands in his hair, and her mouth open. He kissed her face around her open mouth, and he kissed her neck, and he moved his hand in her pants even though the waistband rubbed his wrist.

Then he heard footsteps next to him, and saw the beam of a flashlight, and he saw the beam illuminate the cave floor and the edges of the hay, and then he was blind in the light. He quickly pulled his hand out of her pants and heard Sara Koepke say, 'Danny!'

Tami, next to Ben's face, laughed, though, and Danny said to Sara, 'Here, hold this,' and the flashlight moved slightly off them, and Danny said, 'No, hold it up so I can see,' and then one of his feet lifted and came down on the other side of Ben. And Ben felt his brother's hands on him, lifting him and pulling his shirt off, and then his shoes, and his brother saying, 'Off with the pants, brother!'

Then Danny's hands on Tami, and Tami laughing, as Danny bent down and in the flashlight beam, undid her pants and slipped them over her hips, and Sara scolding and saying, 'Tami? Are you okay?' But Tami was almost hysterical with laughter now as her pants stuck on her shoes. Danny tugged away, his shadow grotesque on the cave wall.

Tami said, 'It's no use, it's no use. You have to take the shoes off, too.' So Danny put her pants on again, turning them right side out again, and pulled them up over her shoes, tennis shoes, which he then slipped off, one by one. Only after he did that could he slide her pants and her panties over her feet. Then he grabbed Ben and lifted him up and lay him down on top of her.

'There,' he said.

Sara Koepke turned the flashlight off even as she scolded Danny and said, 'C'mon!'

Tami put her arms around Ben and held him tight and laughed in his ear, and said, 'I can't believe it. I can't believe that brother of yours!'

Ben felt Danny's hands on his hips, a lift a push, a lift, a push.

'I taught you to ride a bicycle,' Danny said, 'And now I have to teach you to strap it on!'

And sure enough, Ben was in her that way, and she seemed to melt into him, or he into her, and Sara Koepke had walked off toward the front of the cave saying, 'Good god, Danny, c'mon!' and so Danny finally let go of Ben's hips and followed.

It felt awfully good but only for a little while because with the chaos over, and Tami no longer laughing, it was suddenly too silent. As Ben pumped he began to feel very aware of himself, and aware of others watching. Not Danny or Harold or Sara, either, but other eyes in the dark, eyes of the hunters or of the dead Indians, eyes of the bones just out of sight. He kept expecting to hear screams in the dark but heard only his own anxious breathing.

'It's okay,' Tami whispered, very tenderly. Her breath in his ear gave him goose bumps even as he felt himself begin to go soft, and then, slowly, to slip out of her, naked and wet as a baby mouse.

'It's okay,' she said again, and kissed him on the face, and rolled him over, surprisingly easy, rolled him over and kissed him again, whispering, 'It's okay.'

Ben sat up, dazed. His brother and Harold Little Boy and Sara Koepke were sitting at the mouth of the cave. He could see their silhouettes against the starry night. Tami touched his cheek with her fingers before withdrawing to find her clothes in the dark, and pull them on. She found his, too, and laid them on his lap. He hadn't moved. He kept thinking, Is that it? Not disappointed but stunned, feeling newborn and helpless, and still watched by invisible eyes. Tami kissed him one last time under his ear and Ben shivered and smelled the dampness of the rock and Tami's body.

'Don't worry,' she whispered. 'My first time it hurt so much I cried.'

BEN STOOD IN THE PARKING LOT of the drive-in with the gamekeeper. They both looked down at Danny the Marlin on the wagon. Besides turning a marvelous blue, Danny had a huge dorsal fin and a long sword extending from his snout. Ben fumbled with his wallet, pretending to look for a non-existent fishing license.

'Darnit,' he said. 'I thought I had one.'

The gamekeeper let his eyes linger for a moment on Ben. Then he looked to Danny on the wagon.

'Do you not have the slightest idea of the penalty for the unpermitted taking of a blue marlin from the waters of this state?'

Ben continued to search every fold and cranny of his wallet, and not only did he find no fishing license, he found no money, no credit cards, no pictures, no driver's license.

'I can't figure it out,' he said. 'I must have been robbed!' He showed the gamekeeper his wallet turned inside out. 'See?'

'What I see is a man with a grand-sized fish and no permit,' the man said. 'And no name at all.'

'I do have a name,' Ben said. 'I'm Ben Armstrong.'

The gamekeeper looked skeptical. 'And I'm supposed to take your word on that?'

Ben shrugged.

'A poacher's word?'

Ben looked down at his feet, ashamed.

The gamekeeper said, 'According to Rule 39(a), Clause 2(b), Sentence 3 of the Fish and Game Code, I am authorized to blindfold the suspect, bind his hands, line him up against the closest impermeable structure, and shoot him.'

Ben swallowed. 'I must have some rights,' he said.

The man shook his head slowly. 'No sir, you do not.'

'Can't I call a lawyer?'

Again, the man said, 'No sir.'

Ben felt his stomach drop, his face tighten with panic. 'Don't you have to give me a trial?'

'This isn't a criminal investigation, wherein you have all the rights,' the man said. 'This is Fish and Game, wherein I do.'

Ben swallowed, looked around him at the happy burger eaters. He searched frantically for Sara Koepke, for Harold and Tami Little Boy and finally spotted them leaning against the drive-in counter, chatting and eating their burgers. He waved and shouted but they didn't even look over to him. Why weren't they helping him?

'This way,' the man said, and walked him a few steps over to the side of the drive-in kitchen. The man backed him up against the cinderblock wall, still wet from the rain. Ben felt it dampen his shirt, felt the roughness against his shoulder blades. Again he shouted and waved to his friends, and to the other happy burger eaters under the drive-in shelter. But nobody seemed to notice him. Surely they couldn't know that such a great injustice was about to happen. Surely they couldn't know that he was about to be shot for something he didn't do. He watched the man take a step back and open his tweed coat and remove his pistol from its shoulder strap.

Okay, Ben thought, and suddenly he felt resigned. So this was how it would end, the short story of his life: executed at the drive-in. The thought didn't bring the despair he hoped it would. Instead, he had a distinct feeling that something uncomfortable would be ending. Even if he didn't catch this fish illegally, he knew he was far from innocent. He was guilty of coveting his brother's wife. Of adultery. Maybe even of fratricide. Certainly of forgetting too much. This strange trip home in search of love and self-forgiveness had not worked out so well.

Ben watched the man raise the weapon and aim it. The sky was clearing and the day had turned lovely since the rain stopped. The far hills caught the new sunshine and glowed. It was fast becoming a good day to die. *Sara!* he tried to scream, but nothing came out of his mouth. The man clicked back the hammer on the revolver. Ben wondered if it would be the last sound he'd hear . . .

No. Because what he heard next were the squealing tires of a roving NewsVan skidding to a stop in the drive-in parking lot.

'There!' the driver said as he parked the car. He jumped out with his camera, began shooting the big blue marlin in the red Radio Flyer wagon.

A girl-woman (very thin, except for her softball-sized breasts) stepped out of the passenger side of the van. She held a cordless microphone to her mouth and said, 'Testing, testing! Do me, do me! Do me like a doggy!'

The cameraman saw with mild amusement the shock on the faces of Ben and the man with the gun.

'She's got Tourette's,' he said. 'We edit out the naughty stuff.'

The girl-woman positioned herself in front of the fish. A hair person scrambled behind her, brush brush brush. The girl-woman said, very rapidly, 'How about my tits? Doyoulikemytits?'

Then she said impatiently to the cameraman, 'Can we get those guys to come over here and join me?'

Ben and the man positioned themselves on each side of her, and she positioned herself so the cameraman could get the pretty hills in the background with their ninety-seven percent fall color.

'Okay?' she asked.

But the cameraman seemed dissatisfied. He puzzled for a moment and then got an idea. He took from the NewsVan a pink leotard and gave it to Sara Koepke. He asked her to put it on and do a series of choreographed stretching exercises on a picnic table in the background. The bluffs were pretty, but much too still for television, he explained. Movement is what kept people from changing the channel.

Sara bent herself into a series of suggestive positions, most of which featured her round bottom raised above the rest of her. Ben admired her shape.

'There,' the cameraman said. 'Good. If we can compel the average viewer to linger on our channel for even two more seconds, that's major revenue!' He winked at Ben.

The girl-woman turned this way and that next to Ben. 'How's the light?' she asked.

'Great,' the cameraman said.

'Can you see my nipples through my blouse?'

'No.'

'How's this?' She pulled her white blouse tighter across her chest.

'Good. Better. Yes.'

'Boogers?' She tilted her head back to show up her nostrils.

'No.'

'Super,' she said. 'Now let's see if I can get some more of this out before we start.' She took a deep breath and let flow a stream of whispered obscenities into Ben's ear. He might have blushed but he noticed the gamekeeper had moved away and now stood with a growing crowd of gawkers in the shade of a big elm tree. Also in the crowd were Ben's mom and dad grinning and waving. They looked young and happy, casually dressed—exactly as they appeared in a photo that gave Ben his only memory of their faces.

'Shooting,' the cameraman said.

'I THOUGHT I HEARD you scream, Grandma.'

'Nonsense.'

'When Mom died. Or maybe it was Grandpa.'

'I didn't scream when your mother died. I lost my voice except for to cry. I think I cried for six months without stopping. I think my tears made a stream out the front door and down the walk, washed a gully in the driveway and carved an S across the pasture—have you seen that dry coulee?'

'Grandpa said it was from the flood. The year before I was born.'

'Grandpa is lying,' she said. 'I loved him dearly, but the washout was originally from my tears for your mother. The Rio Benji swelled and urned salty that spring. The Old Danny River overflowed its banks. There was misery and homelessness and starvation downstream. There was pestilence and I didn't care. My god. I'm ashamed to admit it, but my grief for my daughters, for Annie and for your mother, is bigger than I am. Do you think I tried to cry so much? Do you think a woman can turn on and off her tears?'

Ben didn't know what to say. He sat on the living room floor. He was a young man but his grandma made him feel like a little boy. Her legs were big, her unlaced black boots bigger. She smelled of grandma sweat and cigars.

'Do you ever hear spirits?'

'Oh, yes! Heavens, yes. It's so noisy in here sometimes I could gag. Can't a woman have even a moment of privacy? They follow me into the bathroom. They murmur and make disgusting noises. They laugh. They weep. Sometimes they bicker like children.'

'Do they scream, Grandma?'

She raised her eyebrows. 'A woman's scream?'

'Yes,' Ben said. 'Loud and awful. It turned the valley red.'

'Did it give you shivers?'

'Yes. Terrible shivers.'

'Oh,' she said. 'I think I know who that was.'

'You do?'

'Yes. But let me pull the drapes. The weather out there is distracting me.'

It had begun to snow outside, big thick wet flakes that clung to the naked branches of the maple trees.

'A long time ago a man and a woman—'

'What were their names, Grandma?'

'I don't remember their names.' She closed her eyes. Her face was covered with fuzz. 'Their names are not important. What is important is that they lived here, in this valley, and they loved each other very very much . . . '

WHEN THE SHORT TELEVISION interview with Ben was over—*Did you kill your brother?* No, I loved him. *You stayed away for twenty-five years; why was that?* Because I loved his wife as well. *Some say you were driven mad by desire, jealousy, and thoughts of murder; is that true?* No, I didn't want to break his heart, or mine anymore, so I fled from both. The young journalist lifted the gate on another flood of dirty words that sent ripples of delight and disgust through the crowd. Meanwhile the cameraman scrambled to set up a shot and interview with the gamekeeper.

Ben used the opportunity to pick up the handle of the wagon and drift away from the drive-in. Nobody seemed to notice except Sara Koepke, who finished dressing behind the screen and fell in beside him. She found his free hand with hers, and with Danny the magnificent blue marlin flopped in the wagon behind them, they continued their long trek to the sea. They walked all morning under the hot sun. They climbed up out of the valley and onto a rocky dry mesa. They passed not a tree, a seed of a tree, or a root of a tree. They could hear dogs barking in the distance. The plain stretched so far ahead of them that after a while Ben's eyes hurt even to look.

'Is there a town ahead?'

Sara didn't answer. Throughout the morning Ben had felt her vanish without a trace and then reappear again without an explanation. Ahead a dark cloud grew like a mushroom from the baked horizon. A rain drop fell, big and fat, *pinging* against the hard earth. Ben hoped another would fall, but another didn't. He searched the sky.

'How far is the sea?' he asked.

No answer. Sara was gone again. Perhaps the cloud had taken her away. Ben's hand had grown tired from pulling the wagon. He could hear the dogs barking but still couldn't see the town. His eyes slipped across the horizon without anything to hold them. Only a few gophers peeking out of their holes.

'Watch.' It wasn't his voice, or Sara's. He looked over and it was the no-lipped old man he'd seen with his grandpa. His great-grandfather Clarence, riding a gray mare, wearing a black cowboy hat bent down on both ends.

'Watch,' he said again, and he raised his rifle, aimed and fired. One of the gophers exploded. The others disappeared back into their holes.

'Bingo,' Clarence said.

The report from the rifle crossed the plains at more than a thousand miles an hour, bounced off invisible mountains, and came back again, roaring past them like a jet.

Ben began walking again. The wagon squeaked behind him. His stomach was empty and his mouth dry and he suddenly didn't care where they were going as long as they got somewhere. He felt afraid that he was stuck in something that he could not endure forever, yet there was no end in sight. *Whom* did he love? *What* did he love? The *mess?* The *journey?* And did any of it matter? He didn't know. At dusk he pulled the wagon into a gully that led to a dry creek bed. The wind carried the sound of barking dogs again, closer, nearby, it seemed, around the bend, and then the sound of voices, men arguing, women laughing, a child crying. They approached a bend in the dry creek bed, and although the air was full of village sounds, he could see nothing but clumps of dry grass, yellow sand, a cluster of tepee rings.

Clarence pulled his mare to a stop. 'I remember this place,' he said. 'From here we chased them through that draw. We're near the river now. We chased them all the way to a cave.'

'Why?' Ben asked.

Clarence smiled. 'This land is our land because we took it. We surveyed it, staked it, grazed it, plowed it, built railroads across it. We starved on it, lived on it, fucked on it, and buried our dead in it. Our crops was burnt up on it, eaten by hoppers on it.'

Ben didn't answer. He didn't have to say anything. His brother the fish had begun to smell awful in the heat.

'How long you gonna haul around that dead fish?' Clarence said.

Ben didn't know. 'As long as it takes,' he said.

'Takes for what?'

He shrugged. He didn't know that, either. He only knew he had to risk sadness and madness—there was no other way. He only knew that what was at stake was breaking his heart and losing his mind.

Suddenly all of his blood seemed to race toward the skin on his right side and he knew without looking that Clarence and the gray mare were gone and Sara Koepke walked next to him again.

'Where were you?'

'Nowhere,' she said. 'I never left. I've always been with you, a part of you.'

Ben blushed and looked at his bare, dust-covered feet. He looked up again.

'Let me take that wagon for a while,' Sara said.

They walked through the night under a sad little moon. In the morning they came to a tree, the first they'd seen in days, on which hung a sign in painted letters,

THE FOOLS ARE NOT ALL DEAD YET!

They passed a string of oxen dead from bad water or lightning. They passed discarded water barrels, sacks of beans.

'Let's eat,' Ben said.

'Beans?'

'These.'

'Too hard on the bowels,' he said, Clarence again. Sara Koepke gone. 'I ain't getting off this horse every ten minutes to shit.'

'But I'm hungry,' Ben said. 'I'm not used to this.'

'Who is?'

They passed abandoned clothes, boots, hats, iron, tinware, trunks, wheels, axles, wagon beds, and bricks of bacon, which they scavenged. They passed a bookcase, which they chopped up to make a fire and boil coffee. They passed gray sandstone cliffs, a coal seam, alkali springs, and hundreds more dead animals. Where the trail narrowed over a cliff, they passed rocks inscribed by pilgrims, and just around the bend they approached a lone woman, weeping, sitting on the tongue of her covered wagon. Her son was sick with diphtheria, dying in the wagon, she said. Her husband was dead a month ago, and the oxen were buzzard food. She kept saying over and over that she saw hard times ahead. She held her forehead between her hands and didn't even seem to notice Ben pulling the wagon with the big fish on it, or Clarence sitting horseback aiming a gun at her.

'Hard times ahead,' she said again, and Clarence pulled the trigger and Ben didn't even flinch to see her keel over and her chest bloom blood.

Clarence dismounted, stepped over her, and pulled back the canvas flap on the wagon. He fired one more time, killing the sick child, and without a word, he mounted his gray mare and began riding.

'I hate suffering,' he said.

'You're a psychopath,' Ben said.

Clarence looked at him blankly but didn't answer. That evening, they came to the edge of a canyon and dropped down to a blue river. Cliffs rose hundreds of feet on each side. Eagles and osprey glided across the blue sky. A breeze moved the fir trees on the far side of the river—a hundred shades of green spires clustered up the broad slope to the top of the canyon. They drank and cleaned themselves, and Ben soaked Danny the Marlin in the water until he looked almost new again, no longer rotten and pale and cracked. His sword was beautifully sharp. His tail an amazing blue crescent.

They made a fire and cooked some of the bacon they'd scavenged. They ate their fill, and when the sun dropped over the edge of the canyon, they went to sleep.

In the middle of the night, Ben woke and saw standing by the fire a scalped man, the crown of his head bloody.

'What are you doing?' he asked.

'Just getting warm,' the scalped man said.

Ben went back to sleep. A little later he woke again. He heard something fly in the air above his head and he reached up and caught it. It was a flying hunk of meat, and it was dripping fat. He ate greedily.

'Hey,' said a voice. Not Sara Koepke. Not Clarence, who lay fast asleep in the shadow. It was Coyote's voice.

'Hey what?'

'You're eating your own anus!' Coyote said.

'What?' Ben said. But he scratched himself and noticed that indeed his anus was gone. He looked at what he had in his hand, and even though he had swallowed part, what was left looked indeed like a cooked anus. He put it back where it belonged and squeezed tightly to keep it from falling out. He blushed when he heard Coyote laugh and it took him a long time to go back to sleep again.

Just before dawn he woke to the sound of bats flying past his head. But they weren't bats. When the sky began to lighten, he could see they were vulvas. He got up and began chasing them, but as hard as he tried he couldn't grab one, only brush them with his fingers as they flew by. They made sweet sounds when he touched them, and he could smell them, and he was almost falling down with fatigue, going crazy with desire, when he finally caught one and jerked it to the ground. He lay on it, his face in the dirt, but his penis refused to work.

Frustrated and exhausted, he listened to Coyote laughing before drifting back to sleep.

The next day, big flakes fell from a flat gray sky and clung to the grass on the side of the trail, stuck to Ben's hair and eyebrows, to the wagon handle and to Danny the Marlin. Snow covered the ground and his feet grew wet and cold, and his hands, already tired, stiffened with numbness. No Clarence, no Sara Koepke, no Coyote. Ben trudged onward alone. How far, he wondered, was the sea? And why had Sara Koepke abandoned him? His feet were so cold he felt as if he were walking on stubs. The trail rose ahead of him and rounded a bend and he paused next to an old man and hooded old woman hunched by a campfire.

'Who are you, pilgrim?' the man shouted in a heavy German accent.

Ben shrugged. He could barely speak he was so cold. He squeezed as close to the fire as he dared.

'I don't know anymore,' he said. 'I'm trying to remember.'

The man coughed so violently that his sword rattled in its scabbard.

'And you?' Ben said.

The old man shrugged. 'Vell, once I thought I vas Napoleon, but now I fear I'm just another dying soldier.'

He coughed again, and the hooded old woman moved closer and put her hand on his back.

'You been on the trail long?' Ben asked.

'As long as we can remember,' the old woman said.

Ben moved even closer to the fire. His face hurt in the heat, and his fingers hurt, but still he felt so good he had to force back tears. He stared into the fire, and in the dancing yellow flames, he could see himself riding piggyback on Danny walking through the wet snow. He'd broken his leg jumping out of a tree, and Danny was carrying him home, and saying, *Benji, don't cry, don't cry*, all the way around the bend and down the hollow to the house, the smoke rising from the chimney, and Grandma in the kitchen crying too. She said something terrible had happened, and she wasn't talking about his leg, even though his grandpa appeared from somewhere, and he was crying too, and then Danny was, and pretty soon Ben was the only one who wasn't crying. Grandpa drove him to the hospital, and he came home with a clean white cast on his leg, but maybe it was before all of that when everything dissolved into an endless dream, the night before that when he and Danny convinced their parents to let them sleep in the barn. He'd been in a bag in the straw, and he woke to see first his mommy and then his daddy kneel down to kiss him goodnight. They were going somewhere, driving somewhere, on a trip, and it was early, so he went back to sleep in his warm sleeping bag in the straw. They kissed him. He'd never forgotten the feel of the kiss or the sweet smell of alcohol on their breath, or the lovely warmth of his sleeping bag and the shape of his parents' dark heads and shoulders as they turned sideways to step out the side door of the barn forever.

BEN WOKE IN A WARM BED in a familiar room. A million dust motes sparkled in the yellow beam of sunshine that lit one neat square of hardwood floor and one sleeping black cat. He got up slowly, tiptoed to the window and saw the gabled barn roof over the garage. He looked below at the empty red Radio Flyer wagon tipped over on the green grass. He heard robins chirping, a cardinal, and then he heard something behind him in the hallway. A muffled breathing, something moving on the carpet. He crept bravely to the door and cracked it, eyed the hallway, and there at the far end stood his brother.

'Nice to see you up,' Danny proclaimed, embracing his prodigal brother, 'Man, you gave us a scare!'

Amazed to see his living brother there in front of him again, Ben grinned wordlessly as Danny lead him downstairs to the living room. But by the time they got there, Ben could tell from the light outside that it wasn't morning at all but already late afternoon, early evening, and Danny led him to a stuffed chair in the living room and gestured for him to sit. He did. Maybe he'd just been napping. He'd taken a nap, right? But that was the afternoon he arrived, and last night he'd bumped heads with his brother in the hallway, and so this had to be the next day. He'd walked to the river beach, right? He was afraid to ask. Sara Koepke brought him a cold bottle of beer. 'I should give you tea,' she said, 'but I don't have any.' She put her palm on his forehead. 'You don't have a fever anymore, do you?'

Ben took the beer. 'I think I'm okay,' he said.

'Take these anyway,' she said, and gave him two tablets of ibuprofen. 'And I'm still sorry about the smell.' She waved a hand in front of her face. 'It's been stuffy like this for days.'

'Stuffy?' Danny said, laughing.

Sara wrinkled her nose. 'He can't smell a thing.'

Danny shrugged. 'You must have got sunburned walking to the river.'

'Then that was *today*?'

They both studied him curiously. 'This morning,' Sara said. 'You collapsed practically on top of me. We tried to cool you off in the river. I wanted to call a doctor but Danny said you'd be okay and we brought you home. You've been sleeping all afternoon. All yesterday, too, and since the afternoon before that when you arrived. We've been worried. All these years away and— '

'Sorry,' Ben said. 'I've had some amazing dreams though.'

Danny and Sara waited, interested, but he stood up quickly to better see the hanging photos of the girls, his nieces, at varying ages. 'My god,' he said, 'they're beautiful. They're grown!' He couldn't help but linger on the face of the oldest, Jessie, looking in vain for traces of himself.

Danny and Sara smiled at each other. Danny's face masculine, friendly, the lines around his eyes and mouth the result of many laughs, the lines on his forehead the result of many earnest concerns. It was a face easy to trust, easy to love. A face that says, *This is who I am!* A face connected by direct strings to the heart without going through the switch-box of irony. Sara looked older than Danny did, but with features Ben dared not let his eyes linger on. Like her neck and her throat, and even her hands. Danny reached out to touch Ben's wrist. He had that habit, Ben remembered, as did their grandma, the reach and touch, the pull on the sleeve. Endearing but often irritating. But not now. He felt relieved right now, happy even, sitting back down in this stuffed blue rocker, sipping beer from a bottle. He felt proud to have such a brother as Danny. Look at him! How he'd thrived and survived and raised children. How he loved his wife. How unvanquished he was! Ben knew twenty-five-year-olds more jaded, more guarded in hope and love and kindness, twenty-five-year-olds whom one might assume by their bruised spirits, their paralyzing fear, had barely survived some great ordeal of suffering.

Danny took him outside to show off his bright new shop. The tools organized in cabinets and hanging neatly above the workbench. A shelf with manuals and notebooks and a fat photo album. On the workbench under a fluorescent light, Danny showed Ben pictures of each of the farm pastures, a photo a month, April through November, for twenty-six years.

Perhaps Ben remembered this project, Danny said, because he started it before Ben left. In fact, Ben was actually in the first few pictures. Did he remember?

Ben looked at himself, a figure in the middle of a blue green field bordered by woods. He'd spread his arms for the picture, but was too far away for his facial expression to be clear. Still, looking at the picture now, he remembered the day, remembered as clearly as anything what he felt that day, how he'd been wanting Sara Koepke, been kept up late night after night with desire. He'd been living in the bunkhouse that summer and fall, helping Danny. They were partners then, or meant to be. But Ben couldn't sleep, was kept awake by his blood racing wildly through his veins, by the thump of his heart. By the anticipation of hearing her knuckles rapping gently on the window above his bed.

'Look,' Danny was saying, pointing. His hands had changed more than anything. They were unrecognizable—large, the fingers thick. As boys they'd always shown each other their hands, comparing calluses. Now, Ben's were white and smooth and his fingers fine. Keyboard hands. The only damage internal, the nerves, the invisible pain. Danny's scars were thin white lines across the backs of his hands and fingers, the thumb nails, both of them, slightly distorted by injury.

'See the changes?' Danny said, pointing. 'See how our most visible problem used to be thistles, and now it's chicory? See this light purple color up high on the hills? This was after a drought and the weed was knapweed, which came from the west, and disappeared the next year when we got rain. I think of that sometimes, when I walk on the soil, how below my feet are seeds ready to sprout tomorrow, under the right conditions, or prepared to wait another decade or two.'

Paging through the photo album of the named paddocks, Mother's Pasture, North Bottom, Tommy's Ridge, South Buck, Fox Crossing, Ben could follow the general improvements his brother had made, the grasses thicker and longer, and the banks of the creek (the Rio Benji) protected from wallowing cattle. He could see the dry years and the good years, and how just looking at the pictures of the grasses made Danny remember other things— about his girls, his children. What they were doing then. The troubles they'd had, the joys. He told Ben how he missed them, but they seemed to be doing fine. Not that they'd tell him otherwise. Oh, they might. He laughed. If they were in something deep, they might. If they needed money, they surely would. But they'd always kept their lives private. He knew they were suffering because the twenties are hard, he said. Maybe the hardest, aren't they?

Ben didn't answer, didn't think he was supposed to answer.

Danny closed the book of pasture pictures, and said, 'Let's go in for supper.'

On the way from the shed to the house, across the yard, a wind touched his skin and he felt a chill that shook him to his core. It even seemed to change the quality of the twilight, to break it into particles of light and dark, and then for a moment everything froze. Even Ben's blood. He blinked and the particles were still there, and the house and the hill and the elm tree in the yard had gone blurry, fragmented, and he blinked again and this seemed to clear the world but the air smelled suddenly different, and through the darkness he could see the lines of manure spread on the pasture across the creek. He smelled cottonwood, and clover, and when he looked in front of him he had to duck under the old laundry line that he and Danny put in for their grandma when they were kids, and when he looked back to Danny, Danny was young again, late twenties, the same Danny that had made love to his wife on the upstairs hallway that morning. His eyes looked nervous, distracted. He noticed Ben looking at him and reached over and grabbed Ben's wrist and squeezed, tried to hurt him by digging in his fingers, by showing how strong his grip had become, and it did hurt, too, but Ben refused to show it. Refused. He kept walking across the yard as though his brother weren't holding his wrist and squeezing and causing pain.

Inside, the smell of chicken baking. The rodent smell gone but something else. A young Sara Koepke waved her hand in front of her face and said, 'Stuffy, huh?'

She'd cornered Ben, and Ben felt the blood rise to his face, and an ardor for this woman that dropped his stomach and almost made his knees buckle. 'Yes,' he said.

She winked and he slipped past her into the living room where Danny sat on the floor messing with his stereo wires. Ben bent over to help but there was nothing to do. Danny lay back and reached to connect new speakers while he talked about a new organizing principle for his ceiling-to-floor, wall-to-wall collection of recordings. Ben made occasional noises but was careful not to ask any questions. Young Danny was a fanatic about music, and if you asked him something he didn't know, you'd only frustrate him. You even had to be careful what you hummed or sang around the house, because if he heard a tune he didn't recognize, he'd make you try to remember the name of it, or the original artist, and then he'd spend as much time as he needed to find it, and if he couldn't find it, he'd learn all about it so he could tell a story about trying to find it, which would prove how rare it was.

While Danny talked, lying on his back, still fiddling with wires, Ben let his eyes wander into the kitchen, where he watched young Sara standing in front of the counter putting food on plates, her back turned, and he could see about an inch of her neck and her hair kept sticking to her shiny skin and the sweat made the tips wet. He was hungry and could smell the chicken but kept thinking about licking the back of Sara's neck.

When they finally sat down to eat, he kept his eyes on his plate.

'Is this undercooked?' Sara asked.

The chicken was pink near the bone but now that Ben finally had something in his mouth, saliva running like crazy, the last thing he wanted was for her to snatch his food away. And besides, he wasn't going to be the one to say it.

Danny either, apparently, because he only shook his head and smiled and continued eating.

But Sara threw down her napkin and fork and said, 'Oh, the chicken!' She looked like she was about to cry.

'Don't worry,' Danny said, slightly irritated, but also, Ben could tell, patient and distant, as though he were used to this kind of thing, and he knew how to stay distant, keep from getting sucked in.

'It's fine,' he said.

Sara leaned her face forward and covered it with her napkin. Except for the sobbing and the jazz playing on the stereo, the house went dead quiet. Danny and Ben were afraid to look at each other. Ben didn't know how long they sat like that. It seemed a couple of hours.

Finally Sara looked up at Ben, a goofy shine on her face from the candles and the tears.

'You tell me, Ben,' she said. 'I trust you to be honest.'

'What?'

'Is the chicken okay?'

She looked at him as though on a dare—did he dare to tell the truth? He swallowed. Forked another piece of chicken into his mouth.

'Just perfect,' he said, and right then he knew he had to go away. In fact when Danny sighed with relief and Sara Koepke reached across the table to pat her husband's hand and look into his eyes, Ben could see that his exile had already begun. That lies had already built a wall a thousand miles thick between himself and what he loved. He knew he'd have to slip out of the house the next morning and leave the farm forever.

Finally Sara removed her hand from Danny's and picked up her fork. 'If Ben thinks it's fine, then it's fine. Let's eat.'

Which they did. But before they finished the dinner, they all slid into their fifties again, aging twenty-five years. Ben noticed first the gray hair on the back of his own hands, then the walls of the dining room no longer covered with shelves of music recordings, but with a photographic catalogue of their two daughters' growth. The chicken had turned to halibut. Danny was talking and he paused to wipe his mouth and his forehead, and his eyes looked tired. He was telling a story about camping down the hollow a few weeks ago in order to bow hunt early, and how he was awakened in the middle of the night by a woman's scream that came racing out of the forest and across the open faster than any woman had ever run. First it was in the woods, then coming at him, and then past. A scream like a woman in agony. He jumped out of his bag and ran around in the dark pasture in his underwear, holding his hunting knife, ready for anything.

'Probably a rabbit in the talons of an owl,' he said, 'but you couldn't have convinced me at that moment that it wasn't a woman in trouble. Except it moved so fast. So fast.'

'The Screaming Woman,' Sara Koepke said. 'You know the story. Your grandma used to tell it.'

'I do?'

Sara put her fork down and leaned back in her chair. 'You don't remember?'

Ben did, but didn't say anything. Danny shook his head. 'Tell it,' he said.

'It goes like this,' she began. 'A man and a woman loved each other very much. So much that they made three beautiful children. A boy, a girl, and another girl. A baby. Does this sound familiar?'

Danny shook his head. Sara smiled and poured herself another glass of white wine. She pushed her plate away from the edge of the table and sat back in her chair.

'Every morning the father would wake before the mother, and he'd wake his oldest daughter and middle son. They'd dress, pull on their chore boots, and if it was winter, they'd bundle up in a warm jacket and mittens, and they'd open the door and walk outside under the stars to the barn. The daughter would bring in the cows and lock their heads in the stanchions, and the son would pour out grain for each, and spread hay, and the man would begin to milk each cow, his face against her warm side. The boy and girl would do their work in the mangers and listen to the *squirt squirt* of the milk in the pail, and they could tell by the pitch when the bucket was getting full, and one of them would take it away and the other would slip an empty one into the same place so there was barely a pause in the rhythm of the milking, the *squirt squirt*, only a change of pitch as the milk streams hit the metal bottom of the empty bucket.

'Inside the house, the mother woke up when she heard her husband and two children leave the house. The door slamming, the boots across the porch. She'd make her way downstairs to begin breakfast and soon the baby woke, so she changed her and dressed her and put her in a highchair. She gave her oatmeal, and she made bacon and eggs and hotcakes and coffee, and the kitchen smelled good, and the yellow light looked welcoming and warm. Soon her husband and two older children came in after chores, chatting happily, and the baby squealed with joy at seeing them. They'd wash their hands in the kitchen sink and everybody would sit down and eat together.'

Sara paused here. Her eyes twinkled. 'Sound familiar to either of you?'

Ben nodded. 'I don't think Grandma ever got around to telling me the whole story,' he said.

Sara Koepke sipped her wine, twirled the wine glass, set it down on the table edge. 'Well, one day a wind began to blow,' she said. 'And it blew the leaves off all the trees in the forest and sent them swirling across the valley with flocks of panicked birds. It lifted shingles off the barn roof and shook the hanging doors from their hinges. In the farmhouse, the walls vibrated, making a dull, monotonous hum. The windows rattled in their frames and the chimney moaned like an old widow. The family woke in the morning as usual, did their chores, and ate together, but they didn't talk much, or laugh and the baby didn't squeal. The wind blew a second day and night, a third day and night, and as much as the family tried go on happily as usual, there was only one thing each could think about: the big wind, when was it going to end?

'On the fourth night of the blow, while the woman slept, she dreamed the wind squeezed through a crack around the window near her bed and poured through her ear and into her head. When she woke in the morning, she could see through her window that outside the wind had stopped. The tree branches in the yard stood miraculously quiet. But inside her head the wind still whirled and howled so strongly that she didn't know if she could sit up in bed. But she did. She didn't know if she could stand, but she did that too.

'Her husband was out in the barn already, as were her two older children, and she heard the baby in its crib, so she got her up and changed her and dressed her and put her in her highchair, made breakfast for everybody as though nothing was different, as though she didn't have a big wind blowing around and around in her head. She held onto the kitchen counter and looked out the window at the lovely new light across the valley, the grasses and the tree branches sleeping, finally, in the stillness of dawn. She heard her daughter cooing behind her, happy this morning, but still the big wind swirled around and around inside her, and she felt it might blow her over.

'She dropped a fork into the sink, and she turned and walked past her daughter in the highchair, across the kitchen to the back door. Outside, she felt the cool clean air on her face, and she walked around the side of the house feeling both calm and stirred to be outside with such a big wind inside her. She didn't know what she was going to do but she had to do something. She walked into the barn, a place she rarely went, and her daughter and her son saw her first, and she could tell by their faces that they were surprised to see her. Her husband glanced up from his milking stool, his face pressed against the side of a cow, and he said her name.

'Still the wind swirled in her head and she used all of her strength to keep her balance. Faster and faster the wind blew, louder and louder it moaned. She could see her family speaking but she could no longer hear their words. She stopped when she got to the big milk pail in the alley between stanchions, and she looked down into the milk, so white, so lovely. White as clouds. White as snow. White as cotton. White as a wedding dress. The wind swirled around in her head and made her dizzy and she felt as if she was going to fall, so she bent down and put a hand on the handles on each side of the pail, to steady herself. She didn't know what she was going to do. The wind was a torment and a pleasure, and she regained her balance, and stood up again, lifted the pail, still staring at the white milk in the pail, white as snow, white as clouds, white as cotton, white as a wedding dress . . . She lifted it higher and higher, up over her head, and she didn't hear her children saying Mom? or her husband say her name. She heard only the wind as she tilted the pail and poured the milk over her head, soaking her hair and upturned face. It was warm and it choked her, blinded her, and spilled down her face and shoulders, wetting her nightgown and her body.

'When the pail was empty, she dropped it, and in the silence of the barn it made a loud clang on the concrete floor. Then she opened her mouth and let the big wind out of her head in a scream. She screamed and screamed, and she didn't need to take a breath for a long time, because what was coming out was the big wind, a long, horrendous scream as big as all of the screams ever screamed in the history of the world. It momentarily deafened her children and her husband as it caromed off the barn walls and went racing out the big barn door, and across the barnyard and down the driveway to the hills on the other side of the road. It echoed back off the hill above the barn, and then down the hollow and back again. Then it raced across the valley to the river, and off those bluffs, and back again. It echoed and echoed, with longer and longer intervals between echoes, a minute, an hour, a day, a year.'

While Sara was telling the story, she'd stood up and walked behind Danny, held his head against her stomach. His eyes closed, face composed between her hands.

'And nowadays,' she continued, 'just about when people begin to forget the Screaming Woman, her voice returns. Danny had never heard her before. Now he has.'

Suddenly it was quiet. Ben could hear a clock on the wall. He could hear a cow bawling down the valley, calling her lost calf.

'Then what?' Danny asked, his eyes still closed.

'What do you mean?'

'I mean, what happened to the woman? What happened to her family?'

Sara still tenderly cradled her husband's head. Her fingers touched his temples and lingered in his hair. 'Okay then. After she poured the milk and finished screaming, after the wind was gone from her head, the woman turned around and walked out of the barn soaking wet and cold. Her children and husband stood speechless, of course, shocked, but the woman felt much better, and how could she explain? She returned to the house where she found her baby eating oatmeal with her hands, happy. She took off her nightgown and showered and dressed, and by the time her husband and older children returned from chores, she had their food ready.'

'What did they say?' Ben asked.

'Nothing,' Sara said. 'Because everything was so normal when they got back to the house, they were afraid to say anything. They wondered if they remembered right.'

'And was the mother okay?' Ben said.

'Oh yes, she couldn't have been better. In fact, by the time she got out of the shower, she felt so good she'd forgotten all about the big wind, and the big milk spill, and the big scream. If her husband or children had mentioned it, she would have laughed, would have thought they were crazy, would have been absolutely certain they were making it up.'

Later, outside on the stoop, after Sara had gone to bed and Ben and Danny had shared part of a bottle of whiskey, Danny confessed that he didn't sleep with her anymore. He'd moved to the couch a long time ago. A year, two years, three. Sometimes she came to be with him, but months passed between visits. He said as bad as that sounded, he didn't mind. He learned long ago that she was destined to be unhappy most of the time. And he was destined to be happy most of the time. 'A bad match,' he said, and laughed. 'A happy person with an unhappy person!

'Still,' he continued, passing the bottle, spitting, 'she's my match, and for whatever perverted reason, she's the woman I fell in love with, and have always loved. My life is full. I played with my girls when they were little. I have good work to do on this place. There are sad and hard things always but I manage to be happy. Just the way the light looks coming in the window in the morning, and you know how I love reading and listening to music. And the way the cows look standing in the grass on the hillside. These things give me joy, make me happy to be alive. New clouds coming over the hills, new air. Seeing how Sara stands when she does something, anything! When she paints woodwork or cooks. God, she's beautiful! And I get to see her, have seen her grow and age, and I've made children with her. She's nuts, sure, and so am I for loving her. But I'm not miserable, haven't been in a long time. Since I learned to keep out of her messes, since I learned that her sadness didn't have to be mine. That to love her didn't mean sharing her misery. And I know that frustrated her for a while, even drove her close to suicide, I think. She couldn't say it but she wanted me to be miserable with her—somehow it made her less lonely if I was wallowing in joylessness with her. So when I finally looked around at my lovely life, the only one I have, when I looked at this farm, my work, and my girls—they were already teenagers by then, almost gone!—when I decided that I wasn't going to be miserable anymore just because she was, well, she almost did herself in. I mean, I walked in on her a couple of times. I thought she was trying to scare me, and maybe she was, and she did! But I wouldn't blink. I told her she had to get help but there was nothing I could do. I had a good life to keep living, and if she didn't want to live hers, well, what could I do?

'God help me!' He laughed. 'I'd never divorce her, you know, or leave her. I know she needs me. She needs me to be here, and she needs me for the joy I take in life, even though she may not be able to share it. She takes her journeys to the dark places, and then she comes back, and I'm here, always, and still helplessly in love, always. It's in my nature, I believe.'

The night air was a balm, humid and perfumed with grasses and chamomile and manure and mud from the wetland. The drier air descended from the big forest up the hill behind them. A barred owl called. Danny lifted his hands to his mouth and answered. The owl hooted back.

Then Danny looked over at Ben in the darkness. "What do want, Benji? You still want her?'

'No,' Ben said. Then, 'Yes.' Then, 'I don't know.'

Danny nodded and grinned. 'You're my brother, all right. For a while there I was thinking you might be an imposter.'

'It's just that when I'm here, I have a lot of . . . memories. And they're not good. I mean, there were a lot of bad things. I'm ashamed. But not just for stuff I did, but for the whole bloody history of this place. Did Grandma ever tell you about Great-grandpa Clarence and the Indian massacres? I'm trying to—I don't know—feel it all, somehow. The whole messy mess of it. Seems like it's time. You know what brought me back?'

'What?'

'Mom's ghost.'

Danny didn't say anything. Ben started to sit down on the grass but the dew had made it wet already.

'She was a white smudge in my room and I realized I didn't remember what she looked like. Or barely anything about them, about her and Dad.'

Danny stayed quiet. The owl spoke across the hollow again but he didn't answer. Finally he said, 'I don't remember them, either. I mean, I've got some pictures in my head sometimes, but when I'm here, on this farm, I don't need to remember them the way you might feel you need to. Just standing here, I can feel them. Not white smudges, but part of the air, the sounds, the soil. I'm not saying I haven't felt their loss, their absence—we were so young when they died, so the loss—the hollow—has become a part of my earth and water and air. I mean, I breathe them, I taste them, I walk on them. Does that sound weird?'

'She brought that letter you wrote, too.'

'What letter?'

Ben told him. Danny stood still, listening. A whippoorwill called from the slope behind the barn. Ben felt the air around him constrict and the whippoorwill called again.

'She said you forgave me,' Ben said. 'She said I shouldn't waste that. So I'm trying not to.'

'Well, if it took you twenty years to read,' Danny said, 'maybe you gotta take more than a couple of feverish days to feel . . . I mean, to really *be* here. To get the best of your demons. You're still half drunk and half sweaty with whatever fever you brought home with you. Are you bitter, too? Is that filling you up?'

'You have everything I ever loved,' Ben said.

'It was never mine,' Danny said. 'It was only a question of space, that's all. We were two boys for a while but men need more room and after a while there wasn't enough for both of us. But there's enough now. That's the mystery. Because it's not that we don't take up space anymore, but we just know there's a lot more room than we thought. A lot more fits than a young man can imagine. Especially here, right?' He touched his chest, his heart.

'And especially if you're not bitter, because I can't do anything about that. I won't touch it. It takes too much space in the heart, and I won't touch it.'

Ben looked up the hill at the rising moon, and then across the valley, and for a brief moment thought he saw a thousand campfires.

'See that?' he asked.

The stars twinkled and the pasture twinkled, and the line between sky and prairie disappeared in twinkling lights.

'Fireflies,' Danny said.

Ben breathed, felt the earth move under his feet. Perhaps he'd been dreaming for a long time. But if there was anything real about his life, this place was it. This was where he began. Standing in this yard with his brother. The night was quiet. It surrounded them. They both breathed quietly.

'What do you remember about Mom and Dad?'

'I remember your christening,' Danny began, 'and how even though Dad came to the church straight from his lover's apartment above the flower shop, how Mom focused on you, on you. I wasn't old enough to understand anything but Mom told me later that forgiving yourself is a long strange tumble toward the center of the earth, toward a place where all is liquid and seething and there are no solid boundaries between us anymore. She said forgiveness is love because it is risking madness by giving yourself away, and forgiving yourself is the hardest of all. She said falling is a natural force and so is being afraid. I don't know. Maybe I'm making all of that up. But I do remember that, during the entire ceremony, Grandma kept tapping my shoulder and telling me to watch Mom's face and never to forget it.'

Ben watched the million fireflies turn to campfires of the Union army and then to stars and then back again to fireflies. He shifted from foot to foot, heard Sara Koepke upstairs, heard the radio turn on, then off.

'So you really forgive me?'

'How could I not and still live my life?' Danny asked. 'Still love my daughters? Still love my wife?' He stepped closer to Ben. 'And besides, there's something else we both know.'

'What's that?' Ben said.

Danny stood right behind Ben now so he needed only to whisper. 'We both know she's impossible to resist.'

Ben shivered. He thought he saw shapes and shadows of starving Indians passing single-file along the fence line at the edge of the pasture. He stumbled and had to brace himself against the porch rail.

'You all right?' Danny asked, taking him by the arm and leading him into the house.

'I don't know,' Ben said. 'I don't know how to make it all fit yet. You remember the bone cave and Grandma's stories about Great-grandpa Clarence? Remember any of that stuff?'

'Easy,' Danny said.

'It's like the very ground we walk on is soaked with blood.'

'Easy buddy. Just be here, okay? You don't have to understand it all. Just spread your arms wide and try to hold it.'

Ben felt a violent shiver and he started to lose his balance but Danny stepped over and held him up. Ben tried weakly to shake him off. 'Fuck off, okay?' but Danny held tightly to his elbow anyway and helped him up onto the porch and toward the front door.

'You shouldn't have got out of bed today,' Danny said. 'You shouldn't have gone to the river or eaten dinner with us, and if you're not better in the morning, I'm taking you to a doctor. Too much sun and too much whiskey, too much of whatever fever you brought home with you.'

'Too much blood,' Ben said. 'Too much for my bitter little heart to hold.' Then he touched his heart, or tried to. He was off balance and would have fallen again but Danny held his elbow and helped him into the house and up the stairs, past the stench of a rodent decaying behind the wall, into their old room. Ben lay down in the spinning bed in the spinning room, closed his eyes and heard Danny close the bedroom door. He listened to his retreat down the hallway. He shivered and curled tightly into a ball and waited to hear Danny's footsteps go down the stairs. Somehow he thought he'd be safer if he heard them go down the stairs. But they paused on the landing. Just before Ben fell asleep he heard Sara's voice.

'I think it's in here,' she said, an urgent whisper. 'There.' Then a rapping on the plaster wall on the landing. Another rap—a slight drop in pitch. 'Can you hear it?' *Rap-rap*. 'Can you?'

DESPITE FINALLY TALKING with his brother and feeling his legs buckle under the true—not anticipated or imagined or dreaded —but under the true weight of his life, the barely bearable weight of forgiveness and his own blood's history, Ben still wasn't quite home. He still had haunts too big to spread his arms around and hold. Haunts he didn't yet know how to endure in his flesh, or to explain away with his conscious mind. For although he didn't feel the same reckless weakness he'd felt for Sara when he was young, he still could neither hold her safely inside nor push her comletely. Age had turned her, changed her, yet he was still moved by her flesh, by the invisible mystery of her smell. He'd been jealous watching her hands holding Danny's head while she told the story of the Screaming Woman. He could feel her trying to get inside him, along with his brother and grandparents, and the farm itself, and all the spirit-crowded air he breathed and blood-soaked soil he stood on. If his heart had been too empty for too long, it was now too full and too near breaking to hold all the love he needed to buoy himself up under such pressure, such exquisite pain. Since the day his parents died he'd been far from home and now he had still more journey to endure, more of everything to imagine if he ever hoped to hold all the possibilities of home again in his heart.

For on this second night after his return to the farm he'd left in guilt and disgrace twenty five years before, after his brother Danny helped him shivering up the stairs and down the hall and back into bed, even pulled up his covers and tucked them in, Ben Armstrong closed his eyes and found himself miserably and relentlessly back in the bone cave, shivering so fiercely now he was afraid his bones would break. Wracked by fever, Ben felt abandoned by family and friends, by the whole world. He was hungry, and felt an extraordinary irritability of the skin, as if covered with biting insects. His guts burned and raised a bitter taste in his mouth. When he lay on his back and raised his knees, he was astonished and annoyed at the strong pulsation of the arteries there.

He had to relieve himself but the wind was blowing so hard he didn't want to leave the shelter of the cave, so he walked toward the back and he stumbled on something in the dark. He fell, and with his hands he could feel bones. He pulled himself upright, peed, then worked his way back to his blanket and lay down. He felt Danny the Fish behind him, and he tried to sleep but the wind carried up the hill the voices of men speaking in English. From the back of the cave, he heard women and children speaking in their native tongue, doomed mothers shushing their children. The white men with guns climbed the trail up the bluff toward the mouth of the cave, and the Indian voices panicked for a moment and then went silent. The cold wind died down and the stillness began, broken only by the occasional rifle-cocking sounds of imminent massacre. He thought he'd never sleep again.

But he finally did, and when he woke a pretty yellow light spread from the cave entrance across the stone floor. He lay still and watched the sky grow pale and listened. No shuffling ghosts at the back of the cave, no stalking, murderous voices at the entrance. Only morning birdsong. A dove. A robin. A jay. Ben turned to see Danny had transformed into a giant manta ray, wide wings and long skinny tail hanging off the sides of the Radio Flyer wagon.

Then he heard a pot banging and smelled bacon and smoke from a fire.

'Good morning!' Sara Koepke said. 'I thought you'd never wake!'

Ben rolled over to look at her. His mouth watered, despite the lingering bitterness from the night before. Sara wore a long black dress and ballet slippers. Her luxurious gray hair was piled high on her head and held with a diamond tiara.

'Wow,' he said. 'Things just keep getting weirder.'

'You like it?'

Ben sat up and nodded. Why not?

'I hope you're hungry.' Sara turned the sizzling bacon with a spatula.

He actually felt much better. He felt no headache or any of the lingering weakness of a fever. So far, so good. He bent down to get a closer look at Danny, who was clean and not putrid. Too cold for flies and decay. Ben touched him, and his skin felt like buttery leather.

'How did I kill him?' he asked.

'A gun,' she said.

'Did you see me do it?'

'No, but I heard it.'

'You did?'

She looked at him, amused. 'A rifle shot in the house? How could I not?'

He stepped toward the back of the cave. No Indians huddled back here. Only bones and the smell of urine, his own. He stretched. For all he'd been through, he felt all right. It was a good thing to wake up healthy in the morning. He walked back past the squatting Sara—she wore a fur stole now—to the cave entrance. Everything as it should be except for the manta ray in the wagon behind him. And his belief that the manta ray was his dead brother. And then the nagging certainty that he, Ben Armstrong, had been somehow responsible for his brother's death. He could see the blue sky behind a blue bird perched among green leaves. He could see sunshine beaming through the treetops to the forest floor, sparkling yellow off the last drops of dew. He could see the blue river bending gracefully westward, then south again. In the distance he could hear big trucks passing on the interstate highway. He could smell the air, clean and moist and full of promise. He couldn't smell Danny. Perhaps he'd merely dreamed Danny turned into a fish, the same as he'd dreamed so many other things. He was tempted to walk away at that very moment—to leave Sara cooking and Danny in the Radio Flyer wagon, to descend the wooded path from the cave to the edge of the river, to follow the trail along the slough to higher ground, to climb up out of the borrow pit — Why not leave? He was a free man. And besides, hadn't he fled this place once before?

He stepped off the cave porch and began descending the bluff. He might have gone a long way, might have made his way to the highway and hitchhiked back across the country to our nation's capital, but before he'd even got out of the timber he felt overcome by a terrible hunger, a gnawing so compelling that he paused when he came to an ox skeleton. Wolves had devoured everything but the flesh on its forehead and face. Ben stood with his mouth watering while he watched another man, a straggler like himself, slice off that part in strips, and soon he found himself sitting next to a fire, watching the straggler (his great-grandfather Clarence, he recognized now) use a large bowie knife to mince the strip of hide slowly, chopping it over and over, very fine, this way and that. The old man looked askance at Ben from under his slouched black hat and fingered the edge of his large and bloody blade with his thumb. He sat like this for a good half an hour, cutting up three long strips of flesh from the dead ox's face, and during this queer performance, Ben cautiously moved a little farther away from him. Clarence put the minced beef into a small tin kettle of water and set it on the fire, after which he put a handful of wet ground coffee from an old dirty handkerchief in another small tin kettle. Then he laid his knife very carefully on the rock to his right, propped his elbows on his knees and dropped his chin thoughtfully into his hands, and began to ask Ben many questions without looking at him. He was frostbitten, and bloated from alcohol, and his questions seemed to be leading nowhere, rather they served as a kind of a warm-up for his own confession, which he was itching to tell. Ben refused to help him, though. He answered every question with one or two words only. Finally, Clarence gave up all pretenses and surrendered to his compulsion to confess.

'Once while wandering in this great country,' he said, 'my partners and me came upon an Indian hut. We walked in like kings and caught the squaw napping. She offered us roots and baskets if we wouldn't molest her, but what did we care for roots and baskets? We liquored up and then passed her around with the bottle. There were five of us and the whiskey ran out on the afternoon of the third day. I sobered up that evening and felt my behavior had been villainous, and beyond the damage done to the poor girl herself, I became quite frightened that a collision with her returning brave would be imminent. No matter that there was plenty of wood, and good water, and trout plentiful in the stream, I knew we had to leave fast, but my companions wanted to wait until morning. Well, that last night I couldn't sleep. Partner Battis liked to beat the squaw. Sober, I could no longer tolerate her screams. So I got up and pretended I was going to leak but instead I got on my horse and rode away. Of course, I felt terrible, but I felt even worse when I found out about a month later that the buck had come back early that morning, when everyone was asleep, and he'd murdered each of my four partners. Only me, for being a coward, escaped with my life.'

The burden of his confession lifted, young Clarence yawned and smiled for the first time. He stretched and leaned back against the rock.

'Of course I also felt glad to have survived,' he said, slumping sideways, eyes fluttering to a close.

'What a big old country,' was the last thing he murmured before sleep.

Ben watched him for awhile and then lay down to sleep too, but before he slept he thought of Sara Koepke alone in the cave, and he felt worried for her and sad to be alone—and cowardly, too. He'd been running from something in the cave—something dark and bloody and buried under all the carefully layered constructions of who he thought he was and wanted to be. How can a man forgive himself until he knows himself?

It was time to go back up. What was in the cave was both why he'd come home and what had taken him so long.

Ben stood and walked up the hill. He found the cave easily in the dark. In the red light from the still-burning coals he could see Danny on the wagon and Sara asleep under a thin blanket, shivering. He lay next to her, under the blanket too, warming her, and she mumbled something unintelligible but tender. He patted the cave floor and located his knife and pulled it close for protection. In the dark he could hear geese high in the sky flying south; he could hear Coyote's laughter and an owl's hoot. Then suddenly a shuffle of men's boots echoed in the cave entrance and from the darkness behind him he heard a child's brief cry.

Ben closed his eyes. Why had he come home? How dare he? Hadn't he known it would blow his mind?

From the cave entrance, he heard the *sha-SHOCK* of ghost rifles preparing to fire.

YET WHEN HE WOKE it wasn't a posse of men with guns hunting Indians that darkened the entrance to the cave. Instead, in the yellow light of dawn spreading across the cold stone floor, Ben saw the shadow of a lone dog-eared soldier squatting quietly.

'What do you have there?' the soldier asked, nodding to the wagon.

Ben squinted into the light. 'My brother.'

'Looks like some kind of fish.'

'I think I killed him.'

The soldier's floppy ears twitched through the slots in his helmet.

'What are you going to do with him?'

'I don't know,' Ben said. 'Once I had a plan, but I seem to have forgotten it.'

The ghost of compassion crossed the soldier's face. Also one of his large, floppy ears. He pushed it to the side again.

'Killing's hard,' the soldier said.

Ben tried not to stare. The soldier cleared his throat, blinked and cleared his throat again as if it had been a long time since he'd spoken.

'I'm in a civil war,' he said.

'What are the sides?'

Again the soldier cleared his throat, blinked for too long, and then opened his eyes. 'Dogs against Cats.'

Ben wanted to laugh but stopped himself.

'I'm serious,' the soldier said. 'Look at my ears!'

'Yes, but—'

'It's the only real difference anymore—a deviation in a few chromosomes. The Dogs have ears like mine and the Cats have elegant tails. We've all lived together for longer than anybody can remember, and most of the time the difference has meant nothing. Ears, tails—who cares? Of course we all learned in school that Cats and Dogs fought bitterly in the last war. But that was almost comic to us. We thought we had progressed far beyond that kind of thing. We thought killing each other was an indulgence of our grandparents. Another weird and awful characteristic of people who lived in black and white photos, before televisions and computers. People whose normal activities were strange anyway— they used outhouses and cooked with coal!—so the accounts of whole villages being slaughtered, well, these were just more weird stories we didn't think about much.'

Behind the soldier, out the cave entrance, Ben could see a train grow long and thin from a spot on the horizon. It whistled and the sound of the engine droned insistently across the flatland.

'So what happened?' Ben asked.

'Frankly, I'm not sure. I remember Rex was elected President, and I remember him condemning the Cats for reasons of freedom and security.'

'What's that mean?'

'Ancient language,' the soldier said. 'Nobody knows for sure what it means anymore besides fear and death.'

The train rolled and rolled, growing like a thread, a thin dark line across the northern horizon. Its incessant moan and occasional whistle grew irritating, menacing, like an unending threat. How long before it passed?

'Then Rex proclaimed this place to be the great Dog homeland.'

'Is it?'

'Sure. But of course it's also the great Cat homeland. And at some magic moment, everyone became frightened to suggest it could be both. I don't know why that happened. I know the Cats started fighting back and their attacks were frightening. But even more than that, nobody wanted to be called a traitor and shunned.'

The soldier seemed puzzled, lost in thought. He blinked slowly as though hoping to see something different when he opened his eyes again. Apparently he didn't, because his brows converged, disappointed.

'Then what happened?' Ben asked.

The soldier shrugged. 'I'll tell you about my town,' he said, 'a small town, the starting point of the front line. It was a stronghold of the Dog army and just across the big river lay the stronghold of the Cat army. They occupied the distant bluffs, from which they could occasionally lob shells. They exploded the oil refinery and also the hospital, which suffered a direct hit. Even the church was damaged. See the crater in front of the cafe down the block?'

Ben looked out the cave entrance and saw the slough down below, and the river, and the train on the distant horizon. He didn't see a town, but he nodded anyway.

'It's a wonder that in these troubled times the cafe is open at all,' the dog-eared soldier continued. 'But everybody needs to do something. Look at that woman washing glasses at the counter. See her through the broken front window? It's winter and there are some frostbitten pigeons on the pavement outside. She throws them crumbs. A few men in uniform stand at the counter. Their dog ears stick up through slots in their helmets and then flop forward—like mine, it's the style for enlisted men. From here the war is a mythical animal that can't properly be glimpsed, only felt. But you can see it indirectly. You can see it in the woman's movements, in her empty gaze, in the way the uniformed men lean on the counter, tilt the bottles to their lips and then wipe their mouths with the backs of their hands. There's treachery in the air, and cruelty, and it has an actual feel, a smell.'

Ben couldn't feel it or smell it. He could hear the train though, and he couldn't believe it hadn't passed yet. It must be the world's longest train.

'Recently I saw my neighbor on television,' the soldier said, 'passing on a message to his own sister that he would cut her throat for marrying a Cat.'

'He's a Dog?'

'Yes, and she is, too.'

'And now he hates her?'

The soldier let out a long, weary sigh. 'The brother says she's betrayed the cause.'

'And has she?'

'Probably,' he said. 'Because the cause is hate. And her marriage to the Cat is motivated by love. So she's now loathed as a traitor and a terrorist, while the brother, who hates his own sister, is universally applauded as a patriot.'

The train, the monotonous rumble, its obstinate advance across the immense plain, had settled uneasily on Ben's nerves. The soldier pushed a dog ear back off his forehead again and continued.

'In order to take away all of the Cats, Dog soldiers needed the help of Dog civilians. They needed compliance and they needed accomplices—so they pulled respectable Dog civilians from their homes, and led them to a neighbor Cat's house. Then they gave the respectable Dog a pistol and told him to shoot the Cat. If he refused, the soldiers simply shot the respectable Dog, dead.

'Then they walked to the house of the next respectable Dog and maybe this one also bravely refused to kill his Cat friend. So, again, the soldiers shot him.

'Two dead heroes lay on the street and the Dog army is unfazed. They pull a third respectable Dog civilian from his home. As you might imagine, this third fellow is more than a little bit upset. Maybe he never liked this particular Cat, but most likely after hearing these two shots he's so terrorized he can't think. He sees his two dead neighbors, and he says, *Where do I shoot this goddam Cat? How many times?*

'This is how it works.

'I was lucky that day, though. I didn't have to choose between my life and a neighbor's. They put me in a truck with other young Dogs and soon I was in the army.

'Here, look at the town. It's warmer this afternoon. See the snowman melting in front of that house? One of the few wooden houses along Main Street that hasn't been hit by Cat shelling. The railway station, the former cafe, the clinic, the shops. Where the doors used to be is plywood. No glass in the windows, just plastic sheets. This street is empty of traffic, few children, no pets. The parson rides by on his bicycle but does not stop. Emaciated and bowed low over handlebars, he rides on because the church entrance is locked and the tower reduced to a heap of rubble. Look at the empty sky, the dead street! Not only do we feel hunger and cold and grief, but also we feel lost. Everything we used to think about and do, all of our pre-war plans—even who we *thought we were*—now seem puny and foolish, and sentimental as a child's dream. Because the hardest thing isn't the dying, or the fear of dying. The hardest thing is the killing. Especially the first time.'

The soldier gestured to Danny the Fish.

'As you know.'

Ben felt himself blush, because it hadn't been hard. In fact he didn't even remember doing it. What was wrong with him?

'My first time it was summer,' the soldier said, 'and our patrol chased a Cat sniper into a farmhouse on the other side of the river. We hid in the Queen Anne's lace about twenty yards from the house and waited for him to come out. We waited all day in the heat, and it was terrible, and we were thirsty, and we knew that any second he would run out of ammunition and make a break for it. I had hunted of course, and I knew this feeling of waiting, of staying still. Of feeling the sweat pour down my forehead and knowing that when I had a chance, I could kill.

'Still, when I saw the Cat at the window, and I aimed, I could not pull the trigger. I lowered my rifle. Was something wrong with me? I'd seen countless people shot by that time. I had him in my sights. I could clearly see his round face, his short, dark hair. And his eyes like somebody who knows he is going to die. I even squeezed the trigger, keeping the sights on him. But I couldn't pull it all the way. Not then. Not that moment.

'He disappeared from the window, and I swallowed, relieved. I thought perhaps I'd been saved, that the next time he appeared would be on the other side of the house, or in another window, and my time for killing had come and gone. I listened to the redwing blackbirds and the frogs down by the creek. I wiped the sweat from my brow. And then I saw him again, there in the same window! The bastard!

'This time I raised my rifle, aimed, and without hesitation I shot him in the head.'

The soldier's voice broke slightly and Ben was afraid to look at him. Coyote sidled past the cave entrance, lifted its nose at the scent of Danny, and then retreated back into the woods.

'The second time was easier than the first,' the soldier said. 'And the third even easier. For a while I counted, but I soon stopped because counting seemed to be a way of feeling sorry for myself. Because I couldn't feel sorry for the dead anymore. See what I mean? Nothing's as it should be. Everything feels pretend, empty, fake. Every breath, every gesture a betrayal of something…

'See that little girl passing on a bicycle?'

Ben looked, of course, but still saw only the slough below, and broad river, and the train on the distant horizon.

'I've known her since she was born,' the Dog soldier said. 'I celebrated her christening with her parents. Her mother is a Dog, so she has ears like ours, but her father is a Cat, and he's been gone since before the roundup.

'*Hello*, she says, smiling sweetly. See her wave? And why not? She thinks I'm her friend, so I'm not going to disappoint her. I'll wave back. But her father's a soldier in the Cat army now, and I know—even as I smile and wave, even as I pretend friendship—I know I might have to kill him someday.

'This is the way it is, the way it's become. The war has spoiled everything. Probably a lot like having a dead brother on a wagon. I'll bet you wouldn't recommend it to anybody, would you?'

The train, which had appeared as a mere dot on the northeastern horizon, had stretched to a thin, dark line with no end in sight. Even after the engine had passed over the northwestern horizon, the rumble of the uncountable wheels, the vibrating steel, continued undiminished across the plain.

Ben couldn't stand it any longer. 'Troop train?' he asked.

The soldier shook his head.

'Munitions?'

'No.'

'Coal?'

'No,' the soldier said, mildly amused at Ben's sudden curiosity.

'New cars? Soft drinks?'

'No.'

Suddenly it occurred to Ben, and he was afraid to say it, but he also couldn't stop himself. 'Prisoners?'

Again the soldier shook his head. 'You're close, though,' he said.

Ben swallowed, glanced at his dead brother, then back to the soldier. The soldier nodded. 'You should see if you can get him on there.'

HE WOKE IN THE CAVE with Sara Koepke in his arms. Her lips made a kissing sound so he kissed them. She smiled. Her breath smelled bad but he didn't care. They were still together and he was grateful.

'You're my hero!' she said.

He felt her against his body—he wanted to remember making love with her but couldn't. She was very young, so young he could barely breathe to look at her.

'What's that silly look on your face?' she asked, and wrapped her arms around his neck. He almost told her about his dreams but decided not to. Instead he pressed his cheek against her breast.

'Tell me what you told me last night,' she said.

'What?'

'You don't remember?'

Ben shook his head.

'Silly boy. You said, *I love you I love you I love you like a fish!*'

Ben didn't remember. 'Maybe I'm dreaming.'

'You aren't dreaming,' Sara said, adjusting herself so that her bare nipple lay like a purple fruit in front of his open lips. 'I am!'

But before he could taste her, four men moved in from the cave entrance. Their boots were worn, their pants and jackets wool, and they carried rifles. He lifted his head to see their pale faces under the brims of their hats. One had very thin lips—Great-grandfather Clarence.

'Shhhhh!' he said, and lowered his head as the four men stepped over him, and then raised it again to see the Indians emerge from around the corner, out of the dark shadows, into the gray light that filtered in from the cave entrance. One old woman held a stick with a white rag tied to the top. Both sides halted, stared at each other, the white men just a step or two from Ben, and the Indians maybe thirty feet away, faces blackened with ash, hair matted with mud, mourning their dead.

'Good god,' one of the white men said, 'they're animals!'

When the first shot exploded, the sound echoed off the rock walls and shook Ben's bones. A child screamed. An old woman fell, cupping the fountain of blood that sprayed from her chest. More shots, then a burst, and soon the Indians were falling all over each other into a pile. Some tried to run and were chased—but a five-year-old girl slid unnoticed along the wall toward a breeze that carried a big black bird and the smell of river. (At the cave mouth—she'd later tell her daughter, Ben's grandma—she slipped onto the raven's back and flew away...)

The white men cursed and shot and the din of gunfire sent Ben's stomach hurtling and his bowels plunging. He closed his eyes and covered his ears but still the bullets flew. And still he heard the explosions and the terrible screaming from the back, and still he saw the mass of struggling bodies, falling, crawling, their human forms changed into a bloody mass of limbs and torsos.

Even after the white men walked past Ben, stepped over him, and cussed as they finished off the last few Indians, even after all of the bodies were finally still, one voice remained. Ben closed his eyes and listened. It was as if all of the cries of the dying had combined to one low moan, one long and terrible whisper of grief. Perhaps it was the wind in the cave, in the mouth of the cave, in the rock lattice that lay back where the pile of flesh had already begun to decompose—he could smell it. He opened his eyes and looked around and saw the bright light of morning pour in the cave entrance and heard the robins and the woodpecker and the dove join the continuing moan.

'Don't leave me.' It was Sara, still next to him, her lips near his ear. 'Please don't ever.'

Ben shivered, felt her hands on each side of his face. Was this their first rendezvous? No, it was their last, and he'd met her in the cave to tell her he was going away, but he hadn't yet, and with the sound of the moaning still ringing in his ears, he opened his mouth to speak but nothing came out.

'What?' she asked, pushing, pressing, pulling, trying to make him ready for love but nothing happening, nothing, he couldn't respond, not with the moan in his ear, the recent screams.

'Can't you hear it?' he asked.

'Hear what?'

'The moaning!'

She giggled. 'Not yet,' she said.

He slid his hands off his ears. 'Can't you hear?'

BEN ARMSTRONG AND SARA KOEPKE left the cave and the pile of dead Indian bodies. They pulled the wagon down the hill and across a wide beige plain toward the horizon and the train. After the blood of the massacre—his grandmother's blood, his own—Ben closed his eyes and tried to imagine washing himself in the sea. His hand ached and his forearm ached and his shoulder and back ached. Danny was beginning to rot again. His lovely flesh had lost its structure and color, turned rank, and new flies covered him.

'A fish gone bad is as bad as anything gone bad,' said a voice next to him. Not Sara's.

'Grandpa?'

'That's some fish, boy.'

'Thanks,' Ben said. He couldn't help feeling pride.

'Where are you taking him?'

'I saw a train,' Ben said.

The sun climbed high in the sky. It baked the earth, and the dead fish, and the two men walking. Ben sweated through his shirt and grew thirsty. Grandpa fell back slightly, and the next time Ben looked, he was gone.

What the hell, Ben thought.

Ahead lay a shining mirage. A Great Lake on the burnt brown plain. The train for the dead seemed to have passed or disappeared. The wheels of the wagon squeaked. Ben had walked a long way and the horizon didn't look any closer. He pulled the wagon down a narrow draw, ducked through tight brush, and then wound his way up the far side where the horizon again expanded before his eyes. He heard the invisible train whistle in the distance and the sound of it echoed not only across the vast empty space but also inside of him, inside his own vast, empty space.

'Am I crazy?' he asked himself.

'You are,' he answered himself.

Then he could hear himself laughing, even though his mouth was closed. He may have been crying. It felt the same. Could all the suffering have cracked his mind and broken his heart? Had the incessant moaning of the murdered Indians tipped him over the edge? Why not completely break apart and float away?

'Give it up to get it back,' Sara said behind him.

'What?'

'Your soul,' she said. 'Or your heart.'

'Which?' he asked.

'I can't remember.'

He was happy to hear her voice despite her incomprehensible words. He wanted to turn around and see her but he was angry, too, at how she kept abandoning him. He felt a lump in his throat and was afraid to look at her for fear that all he was feeling in his chest and throat would dissolve into tears.

'Where are you going?'

'To get Danny on the train.'

She was silent for a moment, walking with him, stride for stride. 'Want some help?'

'You come and go,' he managed to say.

'And you don't?'

They wound past clumps of brown grass. A green crown of an oak tree appeared in the distance and Ben headed for that. They hadn't gotten any closer to the train, but the tree offered shade, at least. Flies buzzed on his brother. Vultures flew circles in the blue sky. Wolves stalked them from behind stands of prickly ash on edge of the forest.

'You were gone for twenty-five years!' she said. 'Then you come back!'

'You had a husband. You had children. What was I?'

'You were you,' she said. 'And I loved you. And you left.'

'There was no place for me here. You know that.'

'But I was never happy when you were gone, ever.'

'Poor you,' Ben said. The wagon squeaked, a hawk whistled. In his head he had a bad little picture of wasted years and it filled him with raging self-pity. He let go of the wagon handle and threw himself onto the ground, face-first. He got a mouthful of sandy loam. He beat the ground with his fists, kicked with his feet. He carried on until he was too tired to carry on any longer. Finally he relaxed, lay exhausted.

'Are you finished with your little fit?' she asked.

'I think so,' he said.

'Good, then get up.'

Ben stood up and the vast country had narrowed to a lush hollow, a grassy valley enveloped by round, wooded hills. No sign of the train. Not even a sound. He felt himself breathe easy. Only the sounds of birds and frogs and a distant calf. The leaves on the trees showed a hint of blush. September—he could feel it in the air, on his cheeks and neck, and in his throat and lungs. He could smell it in the ripe grass.

'Here,' Sara Koepke said, and lifted his blistered hand to her mouth and covered it with kisses. She kissed his stiff wrist, too, and up his arm, which felt like a two-foot-long noodle of pain. She kissed his shoulder and neck and embraced him, kissed his face. She whispered, 'A little farther, only a little farther, and I know a good old graveyard.'

'You do?'

'Yes.'

Ben started to pull. Dusk came quickly, and then night. The stars silver and cold.

'It's got beautiful old trees and a wrought iron gate,' Sara said. 'And in the fall the grassy graves are strewn with oak and hickory leaves, and in the spring, tulips and daffodils bloom along the stone wall.'

'How far?' Ben asked.

'Not far,' she said. 'But maybe we should rest the night here.'

'Here?'

A lovely farmhouse appeared around the bend in the creek, and a red barn, and Ben recognized the home farm. He sighed. 'Yes.'

'Isn't it pretty?' she asked. 'Wouldn't you like to spend your life here?'

'I would,' he said.

'Let's stop,' she said. 'We may know the people who live here.'

Ben pulled the wagon into the front yard, and lifted it up the stoop, through the back door, into the kitchen. Sara Koepke turned on the light—the floor was strewn with dried apple blossoms.

'Look,' she said, collapsing to her knees and sliding her palms across the maple floor. 'Petals! From last spring!'

They slept upstairs. Ben tried to sleep with his back to her, but couldn't, so he turned and embraced her and for a while she was warm and alive, but later when he woke she was cold and had changed to dust that he could taste on his lips and between his teeth. He was afraid he was back in the desert, but soon realized he was still in his own bed, of course, and Sara Koepke had been with him. In the darkness he could feel the dent in the mattress where she'd lay. He could still smell her on the sheets.

'You have just one more thing to do,' she had whispered before she left.

'What's that?'

'Save yourself.'

SUNSHINE STREAMED through the window casting a patch of yellow across the bedroom floor, where an old black cat lay, bathing herself. She interrupted her licking, looked at Ben in bed and blinked.

'Help me,' Ben said.

The cat continued with its grooming. A song sparrow sang on the cedar tree outside the window. Flies buzzed on the screen. Ben smelled manure and dew on the grass, and he heard footsteps in the hall. He closed his eyes and felt a familiar feeling, *déjà vu*, and waited for his door to open.

It did, slowly, and he saw himself as a young man peeking around the door, first just the forehead visible, then the familiar eyes, his very own. Then the entire face, the furrowed brow he'd seen only in photos. He was bigger than he remembered; he filled up more space. And the back of his head was round, and his neck widened into broad, muscular shoulders. Terror flickered across young Ben's face.

'Who are you?'

'I'm you,' he said from the bed.

'I'm dreaming.'

'Sit down,' he said.

The young man pulled up a chair, sat, swallowed.

'Don't do it,' Ben said.

The young man looked up, despair in his olive-colored eyes. He didn't speak.

'Give me what you have in your pocket.'

The young man's eyes narrowed. 'How do you know what I have in my pocket?'

'Because, look at me, what do you see?'

'An old fart in my bed.'

'Look carefully.'

'Okay.' The young Ben shrugged, a surrender. 'You're me. But I'm dreaming all of this. I could make you disappear by blinking hard, by waking up.'

'Then what does it matter? Give me what you have in your pocket.'

The young man reached into his jacket pocket and pulled out a pistol. He pointed it at his own head. He lowered it. He pointed it at his own head again.

'Don't be funny.'

'I wonder what it would be like to kill myself in my dream?' He raised the pistol again, grinning insanely.

'Give me the gun.'

'What does it matter?'

'Because I'm you, don't you see? I'm you and you are not dreaming. I'm remembering this.'

'No,' the young man said. 'If I die, you disappear.'

Ben shook his head. 'I'm proof to you that you don't die, that you live.'

The young man lowered the pistol from his temple, looked at it. 'So you remember being me?'

'I'm remembering being you right now.'

'And you remember what I feel?'

'Yes.'

'And you remember meeting you?'

'I do.'

'And then what did you do?'

'I left the farm for a long time.'

'How long?'

'Long enough.'

'But you came back?'

Ben shrugged. He thought about mentioning his mother the ghost, his grandma the guide, but didn't. 'My life wasn't enough. But it will be now. It could be now.'

'Why?'

Ben thought for a moment. He'd done, he'd felt, he'd loved. All of it. Now he could think and speak, but all he could think of to say was, 'I'm not so afraid anymore.'

The young man smiled madly and pointed the pistol at his own head again. 'Who is? I'm not afraid to die!'

'That's not what I mean,' Ben said.

Young Ben touched the pistol barrel to his temple. 'Why do we love her so much?'

Ben shrugged. 'It's not just her. It's everything. It's this place. And it's him. It's Danny. He's why I came back.'

'Danny,' Young Ben said, and at the sound of his brother's name he began to lower the pistol to his lap.

'Give it to me,' Ben said.

Young Ben relaxed his grip. 'Why does he love *us*?'

Ben shrugged and took the pistol by the short barrel and laid it on the mattress.

'This is a strange dream,' Young Ben said.

'It is,' Ben said. 'And it's only just begun.'

They walked out the door of the bedroom, across the hall, and stepped over a fish-shaped stain in the carpet at the top of the stairs. Young Ben laughed. 'Remember how, after he started to lose it, Grandpa used to leave his fish at the top of the stairs? Grandma always acted as if there was nothing unusual about it?'

They walked down the stairs and then out the kitchen door. Ben picked up the handle of the wagon with Danny the Fish, a small brook trout now that sloshed back and forth in the wet wagon. He pulled him down the pasture, then up the hillside behind the ponds and through the woods to a ridge field. On the far side, under the crooked branches of a pin oak, lay a graveyard.

'Here,' Ben said, and he stopped and turned but his young self was gone, and in his place grew a cumulus cloud, piling onto itself, higher and higher, its flat bottom black and its heights pink with sunset. The wind picked up and turned the leaves on the oak trees, choked Ben with sadness and desire. He stood in the middle of a little graveyard he'd visited years ago with his grandma. On one end, the gravestones stood clean and square and new, white granite. But as he pulled the wagon toward the other end, there in the shadows of the weeping willow, beneath the old limestone wall, the graves became older, the grounds more unkempt, and the stones covered with moss. Gradually, the stones became unreadable, the engraving blurred by years of wind and rain, the stones cracked, fallen, crumbled.

Farther, only piles of rounded pebbles where each grave had been, and then scattered pebbles, and finally only soil and mustard seed and goldenrod and thistle.

The sun turned red on the horizon, dusk fell, and suddenly it was dark. A yellow moon rose, silver stars blinked like tiny eyes in the heavens. A wind blew, picked up speed gradually and soon turned icy. Then the wind let up and the snow began to fall, wet heavy flakes as far as the eye could see. Ben left the wagon and took shelter in a little hollow in the wall, where he hugged his knees and shivered until morning. The day broke warm and spring-like, and the snow soon melted. Ben stood up, stiff and happy to feel the new sun, see the lovely blue sky, feel the promise of the day. But the wagon and the fish were gone and the graveyard felt abandoned, and he felt awfully alone. He walked a row between the graves reading what he could of the headstones. He saw his mother's and paused. Read her name and the dates of her life. He saw his father's next to his mother's, and he saw his grandparents', and he saw the graves of his great-grandmother Elsa and his great-grandfather Clarence, too. His inscription read:

He ventured into the heart of the continent penniless.
He died a wealthy man.

Behind him, Ben heard the sound of digging. He walked that way and on the other side of a blooming lilac bush he saw his grandma turning the sod with a spade shovel.

'Grandma?' he said.

She looked up and smiled. 'Where's the fish?'

'What fish?'

'You never could lie very well, boy.'

Ben felt himself blush. 'I don't know where it is.'

Grandma put the shovel down. 'Listen,' she said.

Ben heard the wind. He heard a moaning. He heard a terrible scream echo down off the forested slope, cross the hollow, and echo back again.

'Who's that?'

His grandmother began digging again. She was good at it, but she got tired and Ben took over for a while. His hands ached, and his arms, but after more than an hour he heard the sound of the metal shovel on the wooden casket. He cleared the rest of the dirt away.

'Open it,' Grandma said.

He was hoping not to have to, but couldn't go against her. He pried the lid off with the shovel. The casket was empty.

'I knew it,' she said.

'Then why did we bother to dig if you already knew?'

'To prove to you something.'

'What?'

'That you're not dead yet.'

Ben didn't know what to say to that. He watched the thunderhead that had been himself as a young man, its black underside boiling and churning. He felt the big wind, saw webs of lightning illuminate the valley in sudden eerie flashes. The thunder threatened to lift him off the ground and put him down in some other place.

'Where's Sara Koepke?' he asked his grandma when they'd found the little hollow in the stone fence. They crouched to get out of the storm.

'She's with your brother,' Grandma said. 'That's how it is. You know that by now.'

Ben nodded. He could feel the sadness in the air, in every breath, but it wasn't overwhelming. It might never go away, yet was there any other way to feel joy? The wind howled through the valley and from their shelter they watched with glee as the big trees danced madly on the hillside. They heard the crack and fall of one behind them and Grandma held his sore hand tightly until the storm finally passed.

Ben crawled out of their little hollow in the wall but when he looked back to give her a hand, Grandma was gone.

Of course she was. She'd been dead for years. People came and went. And he'd die, too. Yet always there were other things. That was it. Always, always. Like how the sun suddenly came out and felt warm on his skin. Birds sang and a puffy white cloud cast a moving shadow across the distant hill. Sara Koepke suddenly appeared next to him.

'Where have you been?' he asked.

'I took Danny home,' she said. 'I held him under the water in the bathtub until his gills began to work again, then let him go in the creek.'

'That's good,' Ben said, feeling immense relief. Dusk settled into the hollow and the sky turned gray. Across the creek the green grass dulled in the new light. A heaviness of shadow lay upon all solid objects. Always, always. There was no loss so great as all of this, no day so enduring.

'How lovely,' Sara said.

Ben rubbed his eyes. Behind her stood the home farm, the white house and red barn. He stepped closer and felt the blood under his skin pull toward her. He felt joy burst through his pores, crack open his skull and leap for the sky. He started to reach for her but stopped himself.

'I didn't know we were so close to home,' he said. 'How come I never discovered this place before? How come we never took a picnic here?'

She raised her eyebrows with delight. 'You did,' she said. 'And we have.'

A FIFTY–YEAR-OLD BEN ARMSTRONG woke in his childhood bed. He blinked back the light, aware in his bones that something terrible had happened, or was about to happen, or both. Nevertheless, his feverish dreams had left him somehow happy. He smelled old sweat on his body and sheets, but through the window he smelled summer. He heard the mourning dove coo and cows bawling in the pasture. He could have sworn just last night it was fall, or maybe even winter. He blinked and looked around the familiar room, listened to water running downstairs, a pan banging and Sara singing. He smelled sausage and coffee until his stomach began to grumble, and then–*crash!*—a hammer smashed plaster in the stairwell.

The singing stopped. A dog began to bark. Ben Armstrong lay in bed and felt his heart beating madly in his throat. Faith and bones helped him sit up and swing his feet to the floor and stand. The mix of light and shadow in the room made space and gave him balance. He stepped bravely toward the door and took the knob in his hand but stopped.

Who was he? A man. A boy. A brother and lover, home again after twenty-five years away. When he opened the door, what would he see? How would his life go? Was his fate laid out like the finite architecture of the house itself, a window, a room, a hallway, stairs?

He suspected everything had happened before, and every moment that ever was or would be connected to the present through his living flesh. Could that account for the immensity of his yearning and his dread?

Yet somehow he knew that whatever he did today might change his life. Even the smallest house contains infinite ways of living.

Danny forgives you, the ghost of his mother had said. *Don't waste that.*

Ben slowly pulled the door toward him, heard the hinge squeak as it opened, and was momentarily blinded by sunlight streaming in the hall window. Downstairs, Sara started singing again.

What's that terrible smell? This wild joy? And what's the past, compared with the future?

'Look, Benji.'

Ben opened his eyes and there in front of him stood the shape of a man, his brother, holding a hammer in one hand and a dead rat hanging by the tail in the other.

'We got it!' Danny said. "We got it, baby.'

Ben felt his chest expand, his heart, his lungs—and as though he were suddenly as big as the world, as wide as the world, he breathed it in, all of it.

David Allan Cates is the author of four other novels, most recently, Tom Connor's Gift. He's a part-time faculty in Pacific Lutheran University's low-residency MFA program, and the executive director of Missoula Medical Aid, an organization that sends medical teams to Honduras and supports community health improvement projects there.

CPSIA information can be obtained
at www.ICGtesting.com
Printed in the USA
LVHW091805140719
624057LV00001B/21/P